GILLIAN SCOTT

Love, Lies & Lemon Trees

A Terrific Tours Series Mafia Romance

Gillian Scott
CREATIVE

First published by Gillian Scott Creative 2025

First edition

*This book was professionally typeset on Reedsy.
Find out more at reedsy.com*

Foreword

Once upon a time, before Google Maps and Wi-Fi passwords, there were the map book and the trusty clipboard. And the person clutching them, usually juggling passports, counting heads, salving a hangover and coaxing everyone back onto the right bus.

That person was me.

In the 1990s, I worked as a tour rep, then a tour manager across Europe, guiding young travellers who were equal parts wide-eyed, weary, and wonderful. Those years were full of laughter, long days, dancing on tables, unexpected detours, and friendships that lingered long after the coach pulled away.

The *Terrific Tours* series grew out of wild, unforgettable experiences from various cities in Europe and creates stories from them. The *What Goes On Tour* series, where the chaos first began, follows Shaz, a tour manager navigating life, love, and a busload of drama.

While the stories are fictional, they're inspired by the heart and humour of real travel life of the time: the camaraderie, the chaos, the crushes, and the constant discovery of something new, often about yourself.

These books are love letters to travel, to the people you meet along the way, and to the beautiful, unpredictable journey that is life itself.

I hope you come along on the adventure.

Gillian

Chapter 1

1st July 1997

The Terrific Tours office lobby looks exactly the same. But somehow, everything feels different, like the room knows that I'm late, three months late.

A slick thread of anxiety coils in my chest as I step through the glass doors emblazoned with the company logo, a grinning frog wearing both a beret and clogs (because nothing screams Europe like lazy stereotypes and amphibians). The doors hush closed behind me, and with them, my illusion of calm. My breath catches. The thread tightens.

I stop in front of the elevator and try to remember something, anything, my therapist said about this kind of creeping dread. My brain's flipping through its mental Rolodex at speed, every tab feeling out of place. The ceiling above me is stained with time and the corpses of summer flies. It's awful, but it's something. Focus. Anchor. Subconsciously, I rub a finger over the small tattoo on my left wrist.

5-4-3-2-1. The Rolodex screeches to a halt. That's the one.

Find five things I can see. Four I can touch. Three, I can hear. Two, I can smell. One, I can taste.

I look around the tatty lobby. Speaking out loud, but quietly, I'm crazy, but not *that* crazy.

I can see: grubby carpet, a frog logo, elevator doors, walls and a ceiling. I can touch, I'm not going to because, yuck, the wallpaper, the watercolour painting of Big Ben, the vase of fake roses and the tiny wooden table they sit in a vase on. I can hear: my heart pounding in my ears, does that count? People talking and traffic outside. I can smell, I inhale deeply, a weird, damp smell. I reach into my canvas tote bag and pull out a small, tampon-shaped plastic tube. My mum repurposed a Vicks inhaler for me by cleaning out all the Vicks and filling it with lavender for just this kind of situation. I pull the case off and shove the tip up my left nostril. I can, now, also smell lavender. I can taste, I run my tongue around the inside of my mouth, mostly minty toothpaste, but a hint of last night's butter chicken. I feel the thread release, I push the elevator button and make my way to the first floor.

'I'm here to see Carlos Stevens,' I say to the receptionist, who barely bothers to acknowledge my presence.

'Sit,' she says, dismissing me, continuing to feed tour reports into a scanner.

'Clare.' Carlos greets me with an outstretched hand a few minutes later. I try to peg his age, mid-30s maybe, the greying at the temples of his dark mop of hair takes him out of his 20s. 'How are you?' His steely blue eyes soften momentarily.

'I'm okay, thanks for asking,' I smile.

This is my third season working for Terrific Tours. The first season, I was 24 and spent the European summer as a general dogsbody at a campground outside Venice. Every day,

Chapter 1

I'd sweat buckets over a hot grill cooking egg-in-the-hole for hungry tourists every morning and dance on a wooden table buzzed on sambuca every night. In my second season, I decided to take work a bit more seriously, and I landed the role of assistant manager of the hotel in Corfu. There I made sure the general dogsbodies were doing what they were supposed to, serving breakfast, dinner and keeping the hotel clean. I'd do the Terrific Tours accounts for the hotel, and once a week, I'd drive around the island with envelopes stuffed full of drachma to pay suppliers like restaurants and day tour companies that were contracted. This year, I was supposed to manage the hotel in Amsterdam, but, well, life got in the way, and as I couldn't get back to Europe for the season starting in April, my job got given to someone else.

'I'm really grateful that you could slot me in the middle of the season, Carlos.' I say as I follow him down the hallway lined with glass cubicle offices until we reach the one belonging to him.

'Take a seat,' he offers, pulling out an orange leatherette office chair for me.

'I'm sorry to hear about your Grandma, Clare,' he says kindly.

Hot tears sting the back of my eyes. I look up at the ceiling briefly, less fly poo on this one, and take a deep breath to stop the tears from escaping.

'Thanks, Carlos. But don't worry, I'm ready to get back to work,' I put on a brave face. 'So, what have you got for me?'

Chapter 2

'I'm glad you asked.' Carlos leans forward, retrieving a worn manila folder from a stack beside him. He flips it open with the care of someone revealing a secret, then slides it across the desk toward me.

Inside, a single photo, sun-faded and impossibly beautiful. It's of an Italian villa, weathered and regal. It sits back from the road, a majestic driveway leading toward the peach coloured building. Five arches grace the facade; behind them are grand windows with shutters to keep out the heat. Manicured hedges and a lush, well-watered lawn surround its foundation, crisp and fresh. Olive trees twist in the golden light, their silvery leaves shimmering in the breeze. Lemon groves stretch toward the horizon, their fruit glowing like drops of sun against deep green. The whole place hums with the kind of quiet that could keep a thousand secrets.

'How does Sorrento sound?' he asks, studying my face.

'I thought we stayed in cabins in a campground there?' I am confused.

Chapter 2

'We did,' he nods, 'but we've been getting complaints. The usual stuff. The showers are cold, the food is bad, and the men are creepy. When I was last there, I mentioned these problems to the owner of Moretti & Figli. Moretti and Sons,' he translates, 'The inlaid wood store that we take our groups to for a demonstration. And Mario, the owner, said he had recently bought a fantastic villa which had been turned into a small hotel.' He prods the photo with his finger. 'Thirty rooms, a great dining room and a large function space. More than enough room for the two groups we need accommodation for during each week, as well as for the hotel's other guests and events on the weekends. He gave us a really good rate. It was too good to pass up, so I said yes! Tours start going there from next week.' He sits back, obviously very proud of his find.

'What will I be doing?' I ask, feeling the thread start to pull. 'It's just that I've spent the Australian winter doing hotel management papers, and I'd hoped I'd be able to use those and get something worthy on my CV.'

'This WILL look great on your CV,' Carlos enthuses. 'You might not be managing Terrific Tours staff, but you'll be working closely with the Italian staff, and making sure that it is a smooth operation will be fantastic for your CV. International hotel experience, hard to beat,' he smiles. 'I've booked you a flight to Rome tomorrow. A Terrific Tours coach leaves there the day after for Sorrento, the last one staying at the campground. Catch a ride with them, jump off when they stop at the inlaid wood demonstration on the way through Sorrento. Ask for Mario Moretti, he will get you to the hotel and show you the ropes. I have the utmost faith in you, Clare. You're the perfect person to take this exciting step in the history of Terrific Tours.'

While I want to share his enthusiasm, he's making it sound like I'm going to the moon, and I have the feeling it's a great step for Carlos, maybe not such a win for me.

3rd of July - 4 pm

Hacksaw slows the big green Terrific Tours coach to a halt, parking in Piazza Torquato Tasso. Sorrento unfurls in a sunlit burst of colour and charm, balconies draped with bougainvillaea, scooters weaving through lazy traffic. Once he opens the door, the scent of espresso and lemon wafts in on warm coastal air straight to me in the front row.

If we'd driven straight from Rome, we could've been here by lunch, but a bathroom stop on the way to Pompeii, a guided tour of the ancient city long destroyed by a volcano and a long, slow, Italian lunch there have drawn the day out.

While tour manager, Mel, explains to the group that they will now have a fascinating inlaid wood demonstration, and of course, the chance to buy souvenirs to take home, I cast my eyes around, soaking up my first look at my new hometown. Before Mel has finished talking, two burly men in dark suits, ties tight at their thick necks, arrive at the coach door. The one on the left motions with his head that Hacksaw should follow him. I watch out the side window as Hacksaw raises a coach locker and the two men retrieve the tea chest that was placed into the locker by our Pompeii guide. Between them, they carry the chest toward a tallish building painted in shades of Neapolitan ice cream.

'Follow me,' Mel finishes, hanging the microphone back in its dashboard cradle.

I wait until all the passengers have alighted, grab my tote

bag from the seat beside me and join the back of the flock. Immediately, I'm hot. Even late in the afternoon, the sun has a bite. I take an elastic off my wrist and use it to tie my long blonde hair up off my neck. I'm glad for my usual choice of natural fibres, my beige linen pants and matching sleeveless top wick away the small beads of sweat I feel forming on my skin.

'This is the most boring fucking thing you'll do all day,' Hacksaw says, matching my stride after he's locked the coach.

'Do the clients like it?' I ask.

'Only if they're looking for a gift for their grandma,' he quips.

'Oh.' My voice threatens to crack, so I opt to stop there. I reach over and gently rub my tattoo.

'But we have to keep Mario sweet,' Hacksaw continues, seeming not to notice my pause. 'He's a handy guy to know.'

The relief on entering the air-conditioned showroom on the ground floor of the Neapolitan coloured building is immediate. I hover at the back of the group as a young blonde woman beckons them closer to her.

'Ciao,' she starts, 'my name is Alice, and today I'm going to show you how Moretti and Sons have been making beautiful inlaid wood items here since 1878. First, the artist draws a picture, and then colours it in.' She holds up a drawing of flowers to demonstrate.

Over the top of the demonstration, at the back of the shop, I see Mel hand a thick white envelope to a well-dressed man. I put him at about the same age as my dad, mid-50s maybe, with more salt than pepper in his dark hair. Mel points to me, and the man nods. Soon, I feel a strong hand drop on one of my shoulders. I jump involuntarily and let out a quick squeal.

'Sorry,' I mouth to the demonstrator as most of the group turns away from her and towards me to see what's going on.

'*Andiamo* - Come with me,' one of the burly men from earlier says.

Every sense is telling me that going with him is probably not a good idea, but I'm in the middle of a well-lit shop surrounded by 40-odd people, many of them strapping young tourists who would surely come to my rescue if I were to be dragged outside. He doesn't drag me outside, of course, he leads me towards Mel and the well-dressed man.

Chapter 3

'Clare, this is Mario. Mario, this is Clare,' Mel introduces us.

'Ciao Mario,' I put my hand out to greet my new boss.

'Ciao bella, Clare,' he responds. Ignoring my hand, he places his own on my bare shoulders and pulls me towards him. He places a warm kiss on each of my cheeks before pushing me gently away again. Unlike my dad, who smells like Old Spice, Mario smells like rich leather and aged tobacco, with an undertone of expensive cologne.

'Come into my office, *bella,* Clare,' he orders. Placing a hand on my lower back, he steers me away from the showroom, down a short hallway and into a large office. 'Sit,' he pulls out an ornately carved, dark wood chair with a thick red cushion on the seat for me. '*Uno momento.*' Mario raises a finger to indicate he will be back in one minute and ducks back out of the office.

In his absence, I look around. Across the wide desk in wood matching my chair is another, but with grander proportions. Behind the chair, a long painting hangs on the frescoed wall. Inside a thick gold frame, the artwork showcased reminds me of the Last Supper, but the apostles are replaced with Italian men of varying ages, all wearing suits, and in the middle, instead of Jesus, is Mario. Many of the men smoke cigars, a few hold glasses of an amber coloured alcohol. On the table is a banquet, platters of food, plates with meals half eaten, more glasses of alcohol and a couple of revolvers lay on the white tablecloth, their barrels pointed towards the artist.

Odd combo.

To my right is a large picture window with a view over Piazza Torquato Tasso. Behind me, the wall is lined with bookshelves. Sections of leatherbound books are interspersed with artefacts, many of which look similar to what we viewed earlier on our tour of Pompeii. A couple of framed photographs show a younger Mario, a beautiful woman with dark hair by his side. In front of them are two adorable dark-haired children.

'Coffee?' Mario asks, placing a shot of espresso in front of me before I can respond.

'Thank you.' I take a sip to be polite. Almost immediately, my heart starts to race and I feel the thread of anxiety start to tighten. This is why you don't drink coffee, Clare, I remind myself.

'So, Clare, let me tell you about Villa delle Palme, the villa of the palms,' Mario beams proudly. 'While we have owned Moretti and Sons and been making inlaid wood since 1878, we have only gone into the hotel business this year. Villa delle Palme has 30 guest rooms and staff quarters in the old stable for two. You will have one room, and the hotel receptionist, Paola, will have the other. You will have a private bathroom and all the food you want to eat from the kitchen.'

'Sounds good, I smile.' Reaching into my tote bag, I retrieve my bottle of water and take a long drink to try and dilute the caffeine. 'And what will I be doing exactly?' I reach back into my tote bag, retrieve my notebook and a pen and prepare myself to take notes.

'You're keen to get into it, *molto bene*. You will work closely with Paola. There will be one Terrific Tours group arriving on Monday and another on Wednesday. Both stay for two nights. The itinerary for them in Sorrento is to stop first here to buy inlaid wood. The tour manager pays me for the optional Capri Island tour and an optional dinner at Bussola Sud. Then they go to the hotel, check in and relax for a bit. After the tour manager will walk them downhill to the optional dinner. When they stay at the campsite, they have to drive, but Villa delle Palme is much closer. An easy 15-minute walk downhill. Not so much back after cocktails,' he laughs. 'At Bussola Sud, those who have opted in get dinner, can try some local cocktails, dance and even do karaoke if they want. The passengers pay for taxis back to the villa, 30,000 lira. They give money for the taxi to the bar staff and they organise the taxi for them so they don't get ripped off.'

'Uh huh.' I make a noise to indicate I'm following, my head is down, and my hand is moving quickly across the page. I'm sure Mario is clipping the ticket with the boat, the bar and the taxi's but I keep that an inside thought.

The Italian police require the hotel to hold passports of foreigners, usually. We can get around this by taking a list of passport numbers and holding the passport of just the tour manager. Okay? The next day, the driver takes the group to Marina Piccola, and he will then bring the coach back here. The tour manager pays cash at the ticket office for the boat trip to and from the island of Capri. You can go on the trip tomorrow with Mel and Hacksaw, so you can see how it works. Paola will phone the boat ticket office each morning when a tour is going and let them know how many tickets are needed. The boat leaves at 9 am and comes back at 3.30 pm. After a day on Capri, the group go back to the villa for dinner. The next day, they leave early for Brindisi.' Mario sits back in his enormous chair. 'Any questions?'

'What is it that I will be doing?' I ask. Everything Mario has mapped out seems to be easily handled by a tour manager, driver and the hotel receptionist.

'*Si!* Of course, sorry, I should have explained. Terrific Tours wouldn't sign the contract unless we agreed they could have a staff member on site to ensure everything is running smoothly. I think you can help Paola with invoicing Terrific Tours and by making sure all the Terrific Tours bookings are in the hotel booking system. *Bene*?' Mario asks.

I nod on the outside, all calm and collected, but inside I'm burning. Bloody Carlos has thrown me to the wild dogs. The 'work' Mario has described sounds like it will take all of an hour a week. What am I going to do for the rest of the time? Paint my nails? Read books? Sit around worrying that my career is going nowhere? Think about all the study I've wasted?

Mario cuts through my thoughts. 'Can you ride a motorini?'

'Um.. A motor scooter? I used to have one when I was a teenager to get around Wallan. That's my hometown,' I explain.

'*Perfecto!* I am loaning you a motorini to get around your *new* hometown,' he smiles. 'Follow me.'

Mario leads me out the back door to a side street lined with motorinis in muted shades of blue, brown, and black. At the end of the row, one bright orange one stands out like the proverbial dog's balls.

'*Questo*,' he says, pointing to the orange one. He pulls a key out of the pocket of his tailored trousers, unlocks the seat, lifts it and retrieves a helmet of the same colour. 'It's automatic so *infallibile*.'

'Lovely,' I lie as he plonks the helmet on my head and reaches under my chin to secure it.

I'm going to look like a fucking moving salad bowl.

Mario places the key in the slot, turns it, and the engine bursts into life. 'Wait here for a minute. I will come past soon in a red car, then follow me.'

'What about my luggage?' I yell, the helmet making me unaware of my volume.

'Already in my car.'

Tentatively, I sit on my new mode of transport. I hoist my tote bag higher on my shoulder, then decide it will be safer, for both it and me, if I place it between my feet. I lower it, hooking the strap over the knee of the leg already resting on the footboard. I put my hands on the grips and examine the controls. I twist a handle, giving it a rev, test the brake levers and turn on and off the indicators. Finally, I push the horn button. 'MEEHHHRP!' erupts from my tangerine dream. A sound louder than you'd expect from something this size, like a startled goose with a megaphone. It cut through the buzz of traffic and made a couple of pigeons flap off in alarm. 'Sorry,' I mouth to a couple of women who happened to be crossing the road. They glare back at me angrily before disappearing into the shade just as Mario pulls up alongside me.

He winds down the passenger window, 'follow me.' He says, and he's off. He doesn't ease me into driving on the wrong side of the road on a bike I haven't handled for nearly 10 years. No. He takes off at full Italian speed, whipping into a U-turn and heading back down the one-way street, this time, the wrong way. I push the motorini off its stand and tentatively get into his slipstream. He makes a left onto Viale Enrico Caruso; thankfully, the middle of this road is lined with trees, with our lane only wide enough for one car, and the one in front of him is moving at a snail's pace. The road bends, the median vanishes, and it narrows to a single lane, though traffic still flows both ways. I keep as far to the right as I can to avoid oncoming traffic that sways as cars in both lanes avoid each other, but also focus on not clipping any pedestrians walking on the narrow footpath with my prominent wing mirrors.

Without indicating, Mario ditches the slow car in front, taking a sharp left onto Via Fuorimura, which is not only narrow but steep. The engine of my tangerine dream strains on full throttle to keep up with the red car in front, which is getting smaller every second as it powers away. When the road hits a T junction, I look frantically both ways, trying to spot Mario. I see him in the distance to the right. I power off, push my head forward and hope that gives me a bit more speed. Thankfully, traffic slows his progress again and allows me a chance to catch up before he makes a left onto Via Parsano. So far, I'm unimpressed; all we have passed are rows and rows of low-level apartments. When Via Parsano veers to the left, Mario swerves right, narrowly avoiding a bus, as he speeds onto Via Sant'Antonio. The scenery improves the higher we climb. To my left now is a long, very old-looking stone wall and to my right, some kind of horticulture, olives? The wind in my face and having to focus on the road make it too hard to tell. I wish I could ask Mario how much further. My accelerator hand is getting tired. As if he's reading my mind, the brake lights flash on the car, it slows and turns right into a driveway.

What I see when I also turn takes my breath away.

Chapter 4

The land slopes away from the road, and a wide pebbled driveway leads down to one of the most beautiful buildings I've ever seen. Either side of the driveway, gnarled olive trees, topped with silvery green foliage, lead my eyes down to the villa. The photo Carlos showed me didn't do justice to the grand building, its peach-toned walls glowing in the afternoon sun. In front of the building is a pebbled forecourt which will be perfect for turning or parking a bus.

I slow my motorini to a crawl, keen to avoid losing control and tipping over at this late stage. I breathe in deeply, the air is heavy with the earthy scent of sun-warmed olive trees, dusty, green, and grounding, layered with the sharp, bright zing of lemons ripening on the branch. There's a hint of citrus blossom in the breeze, soft and floral, carried on warm air that smells faintly of dry stone and distant sea salt. It's the kind of scent that I think will become ingrained in my memory, fresh but ancient, and unmistakably Mediterranean. I pull up beside Mario and turn off the ignition, and pull the motorini back onto its stand, grateful to have made it in one piece.

'What do you think?' Mario asks.

'Oh, Mario, it's beautiful. Our guests are going to love it here!' I reply with an eagerness that I didn't expect to be feeling. I pick up my tote bag, remove my helmet, and place it on the footboard where the bag was.

'Let me show you around the grounds, then I'll take you inside.' Mario says, moving towards the side of the building. Attached to the side of the villa is another structure, its roof lowest where it joins the side of the main building, rising as it moves towards the olive trees. Mario leads me into the side building's open French doors. 'This used to be the Limonaia,' he explains.

'What's a limonaia?' I ask as I look around the beautiful space.

To our right, a peach-and-beige stone wall connects to the main building, made entirely of the same sun-warmed material. On the left, the high wall is broken by vast, metal-framed windows, most are swung open to welcome the gentle sea breeze drifting uphill. The slanted ceiling is lined with honey-toned timber, supported by massive matching beams. Along the walls, on the worn concrete floor, lemon trees in terracotta pots add splashes of green and yellow.

'It's where traditionally the owners of the villa would have grown their lemons. Sorrento lemons are famous, you know,' he boasts. 'The oil-rich peel makes the best limoncello. Now, we can use this space for functions, weddings, anything.'

We exit through the opposite end onto a tree-lined path that takes us to the rear of the building. A swimming pool surrounded by wooden deck loungers sparkles, welcoming guests to cool off. Past the swimming pool is a small stone building with two large, wooden doors. Mario leads me towards it, pulls a wooden sliding lock aside and opens it.

'Your new home,' he says, finding a light switch and flicking it on. The thick stone walls keep the inside cool, even after this hot Sorrento day. I step into a small lounge area, complete with an overstuffed couch facing a cabinet with a TV on top. 'Only Italian channels,' Mario tells me. In an alcove to the right is a kitchen bench with a sink and a bench-top oven, and a small refrigerator hums quietly in the corner. There are three worn wooden doors off the lounge. 'Go ahead,' Mario indicates I should explore.

I push open the door furthest away, 'Wow,' is all I can say. A cosy bedroom with a double bed raised high off the concrete floor by four solid carved wooden legs rests against the middle of the far wall on the left. Opposite it is a wooden wardrobe, two doors, both featuring mirrors. On the far side of the room, a small window looks out over more olive groves, down over Sorrento and to the ocean. The bed is dressed with an offwhite linen duvet cover, and the numerous pillows are covered in crisp white cotton. Across the bottom of the bed, a folded blanket adds a pop of sky blue.

'Your luggage will be here soon. Later, you can settle in,' Mario smiles.

I leave the bedroom and ease open the next door, but nothing prepares me for the blow of beauty that is the bathroom; it hits like a sucker punch to the chest. The far wall is dominated by an arched window much larger than the one in the bedroom, flanked by rustic wooden shutters that promise privacy without stealing the view. And what a view, rolling hills, olive groves, and the glitter of the distant sea, now framed like a Renaissance painting. Below it, a deep, high-sided copper bath gleams invitingly, perfectly positioned so you can soak in the scenery as much as the water. The taps, in a country style and separate from the tub, include a handheld shower with a design as elegant as it is functional. A marble-topped basin and a simple toilet complete the room, all set atop warm terracotta tiles that seem to glow in the soft afternoon light. It's not just a bathroom - it's a sanctuary.

'I can't wait to see what's behind door number three,' I say as I leave the bathroom.

'Oh, this is the adjoining door to the next apartment, Paola's. You can both decide whether you have it open for visits or keep it locked for privacy. Come inside and I'll introduce you.' Mario leads the way out of my new home.

If the Wild Dogs of Wallan could see me now, I smile to myself, before a shiver of trauma slithers down my spine. It's the first time in a while I've thought about the pack of girls who made my life a living hell for three years in primary school, the ones who kick-started my anxiety. I quickly shake the thought of them away. Mario leads me around the swimming pool, up a flight of stone steps, across the villa terrace dotted with small cafe-style tables, chairs and umbrellas, and through more grand French doors.

'This is the dining room. It seats about 60 people at once if we need,' he explains quickly, then moves towards the swinging doors on our right.

My eyes flick around, trying to take it all in. The double-height ceiling gives the room an airy, open feel. At the far end, a massive fireplace commands attention. Candle-style sconces cast a soft glow over walls washed in a dusty olive-earth hue, somewhere between terracotta and tawny gold, like the soil of the grove after a long, hot summer. Rustic-chic tables and chairs line the room atop glossy oatmeal-toned tiles, while a few potted palms provide the only splash of greenery.

The swing of the doors snaps me back to attention, and I follow Mario into an industrial kitchen. In the centre, stainless steel prep benches are cluttered with chopping boards, knives, and vegetables waiting to be sliced. Wielding one of the knives is a small, solidly built woman with grey hair knotted in a bun. Her makeup-free face is set with focus, and a white apron covers a faded, floral-print dress. The grip of her hand on the blade speaks of a life shaped by hard work.

'Ciao zia Anna,' Mario greets her. 'This is my Aunt Anna,' he says to me. 'She is the villa's cook. Anna, this is Clare.' Mario switches to Italian at machinegun speed, '*È lei quella con cui dobbiamo fare i conti durante l'estate per fare i tour* (She is the one we have to put up with for the summer to get the tours).'

'Si,' Anna grunts. 'Clara?' she asks, giving me the once-over.

I make a quick mental note to learn Italian.

'Ciao Anna, nice to meet you,' I smile. 'Clare.'

'I call you Clara, the other one too hard.' Anna swings the knife, bringing it down loudly onto the chopping board, decapitating an innocent carrot.

'You will meet the grandsons of my Aunts, Rocco, who is the barman, and Nico, who is the handyman, later. Also, my Aunt Maria, Rocco's nonna, who is the cleaner,' Mario explains as he leads me out of the kitchen and down a wide hallway that leads to an atrium at the front of the building.

'This really is a family business, huh?' I say, soaking in my surroundings.

'Through those doors on the right is the bar,' Mario says, veering left and dodging my statement. With the hotel's grand front door in front of us, to our left stands a long modern reception desk with two computer screens. Behind one of the screens sits a woman around my age, oozing classic Italian style, long, glossy black hair, pouty lips, and glasses that might be more fashion than function. She glances up, pushing them higher on her strong nose with a perfectly manicured red fingernail.

'Ciao, Mario,' she says, languidly standing and moving towards me with her hand outstretched. 'Ciao, I'm Paola. It will be a pleasure to be working with you,' she says, her English perfect.

'Ciao, Paola,' I clasp her elegant hand in mine. 'I'm really looking forward to working with you.'

'Bene,' Mario says, seemingly pleased with his tour. 'I'll leave you two to get to know each other. Clare, tomorrow you park your motorini back at the shop and walk to the dock to meet Mel and her group. Be there by 8.30 am. Oh, and don't forget to take your *costume da bagno*. Paola, how do you say in English?'

'In Australian, cossie,' Paola smiles warmly. In that moment, I knew we were going to get along.

Chapter 5

8 am

The ride down to Piazza Torquato Tasso is far more civilised than yesterday's uphill Grand Prix. Well-rested after a glorious night in my new bed, I tilt my chin to the sun like a smug lizard on a hot rock, soaking in the morning breeze and feeling very much on the right side of fabulous.

Parking my tangerine dream back on the end of the line of mopeds across the road from Moretti and Sons, I sling my very full tote bag over my shoulder after retrieving a floppy sunhat and my sunglasses out of it. With a pep in my step, I stroll down Via Luigi de Maio following the start of its sharp S-bend as it descends to Marina Piccola. I cut across on the pedestrian path, ducking down stairs that indicate they lead to the ticket office. When the space opens up, I spot Mel, her group gathered around her. I join the back of the group and listen in.

'I'm going to hand you each a ticket,' Mel shouts. 'Please don't lose it, this is also your ticket home. The boat home leaves at 3.30 pm, that's half past three. It's your responsibility to get back to the port on time. The 20 of you doing the island boat tour will stay with me when we get off at the other side. We will then go on another boat that takes us around the island. During this tour, if the weather and the waves allow, you will have a chance to go into the famous Blue Grotto. This will cost 10,000 lira. Please make sure you have the right change ready if possible. The 15 of you who are not doing the boat tour will have free time on Capri until 3.30 pm. You might want to catch one of the shuttle buses up to Anacapri, have a look at the shops, and have some lunch or just lie on the beach all day; the choice is yours. You can catch a bus from there to the Blue Grotto if you want, from memory it costs about 16,000 lira. Any questions?' Mel asks. I refrain from putting my hand up and asking what time the return boat leaves or where I should have lunch. 'Okay, follow me,' Mel orders. She turns and leads her flock, and me, to a boat called 'The Paolo'.

'Where's Hacksaw?' I ask after we set sail for the 45-minute trip.

'Gone back to bed, I imagine,' Mel rolls her eyes.

'Big night?' I laugh.

'For both of us. At least he managed to drop us down to the port, and I have you to keep me company, so I'm happy,' Mel smiles.

By 10 am, Mel, 20 of her flock and I have transferred to a smaller craft and have set off to circumnavigate the island. The water around the Isle of Capri shimmers in surreal shades of turquoise and sapphire, so clear it looks as if the island is floating on liquid glass. As we motor slowly around the shoreline, I slip off my shorts and singlet top, enjoying the feeling of the sun hitting skin that is not covered by my lime green bikini. 'Want me to rub sunscreen on your back?' Mel offers, waving a bottle of Bain de Soleil in my direction.

As we near midday, I've resorted to redressing and have moved to the shade of the cabin, my skin already tingling and a bit red. The boat slows and stops outside a cave entrance. A flotilla of white row boats, each accented with stripes of sky blue, deep red or sunshine yellow and with older, tanned men in charge of the oars, surrounds The Paolo. I venture back into the sunlight, 10,000 lira held tightly in my hand and wait my turn to be ushered onto a boat. After I make the treacherous leap from big boat to small boat, I hand the tattered blue note to the oarsman and find a spot on one of the narrow bench seats.

'I'm Salvatore,' the oarsman says to me and two girls from Mel's tour as he stands in the middle of the boat, balancing like a pro. 'No sit bench, sit floor.' He points to the bottom of his boat. We shuffle off the wooden bench onto the boat's floor. The seat of my shorts is instantly soaked, not from excitement, but from the seawater sloshing back and forth as the boat rocks on the swell. 'We go,' he says, digging his oar into the blue water, dragging us towards a crowd of boats, and the entrance to the grotto. It's manic and chaotic. Boats bob around waiting for their turn. Tourists who have arrived down the steep rock stairs are taking their lives in their hands when transferring to the small boats.

Once we've edged to the front of the line, Salvatore says, 'When I say duck, you duck. Okay? DUCK!'

As the water lowers for a moment, Salvatore grasps a rope leading into the grotto, lowers himself backwards so his head is almost in my lap and pulls us forward as I try to duck my head below the side of the boat. When he pops upright again, we have made it through the narrow entrance and are inside the most magical landscape I have ever seen. The vast cave is lit by an eerie blue glow, the water a deep, vivid shade of lapis lazuli, like something you'd see in a piece of antique jewellery, not lapping at the sides of a boat.

'*Bella*, no?' Salvatore asks, and all we can do is nod in response as he bursts into song.

'Ma n'atu sole cchiù bello, oi ne'
'O sole mio sta nfronte a te!
'O sole, 'o sole mio
Sta nfronte a te, sta nfronte a te!'

His deep baritone notes echo around us, adding to the wondrous spectacle.

The rest of the day tries to live up to the Blue Grotto, but it's a tough act to follow. The rickety bus ride to Anacapri is hair-raising, screeching around hairpin bends, flirting with cliffs and sheer drops. The town is peaceful, with stunning views over the Bay of Naples, but as I board the 3:30 pm boat back to Sorrento, the first note I jot down is: Everyone must see the Blue Grotto.

...

5 July - 8.30 am

After a sit-down shower in my beautiful copper bathtub, I dress ready for a solid day's work, whatever that might look like here. I match a crisp, white cotton shirt with a pair of sage green linen pants. I stare at myself for a moment in the bathroom mirror. Is it my imagination, or do I look like a more relaxed version of myself that landed in London less than a week ago? The sun has brought out the faint freckles across my nose, and the dark circles beneath my green eyes, once a constant reminder of the long months supporting Mum through Grandma's illness and then our shared grief, seem to have faded. I gather a section of hair from either side of my face and twist it back, securing it with a jaw clip to keep it out of my eyes. Right then, let's do this.

I wander into the kitchen to find Anna once again wielding a knife, this time expertly slicing apples and oranges for a serving plate. Beside her, a slightly older version of Anna leans on a mop, chatting animatedly as if scrubbing floors and gossiping were one seamless task. They stop talking when they see me and stare.

'Ciao, Anna,' I greet the cook. 'And you must be Maria?'

'*Si*,' she snaps.

Sensing I'm not going to get any conversation going, I bid the sisters farewell and go in search of Paola. I find her in the atrium watering the many potted palms that decorate the area.

'*Ciao*, Clare,' she greets me. 'How did you sleep?'

'Well, thank you, and you?'

'*Bene, grazie*. Are you ready to get to work?' Paola asks.

'Sure am,' I smile, taking out my notebook so I look ready.

'First, we have coffee. ANNA,' she yells down the hallway, '*DUE CAPPUCCINI PER FAVORE*.'

'Oh, I don't drink coffee,' I stutter.

'This is not coffee,' Paola reassures me, 'it's cappuccino. Come.'

'So why don't you drink coffee?' Paola asks me after we've collected cups from Anna and selected a table on the back patio.

'I find the caffeine makes my anxiety worse,' I say cautiously, not sure how much to reveal to my new workmate.

'What do you have to be anxious about?' Paola teases. 'You are living in the gateway to the Amalfi Coast, in a beautiful villa with the rest of the summer stretching out ahead of you. Maybe you find a nice Italian boyfriend who can help you fill in time AND make you less anxious,' she winks. 'Speaking of which,' she turns my attention to the garden.

An Adonis of a man is vacuuming the pool, shirtless, his torso carved like marble and a trail of dark hair leading from his navel into the waistband of impossibly cool, low-slung, stonewashed jeans. The only thing he wears besides those jeans? A pair of classic Ray-Ban Wayfarers, hiding whatever mischief might be in his eyes.

'NICO,' Paola shouts. 'Come, meet Clare.'

Languidly, Nico sets the long handle of the vacuum against the edge of the swimming pool and ambles up to us. I'm glad it's slow, as it gives me time to wonder what it would be like to lick that stomach. I feel heat rushing up my neck at the thought.

'*Ciao*, Clare,' Nico says before lowering his face to mine and gently kissing each of my cheeks, achingly close to the corners of my mouth.

'Hey, stop snogging the staff,' another male voice says. Turning, I see Nico's clone approaching, but this one is fully dressed. A vintage rock t-shirt covering whatever lies under it, tucked into a pair of dark jeans.

'This is my cousin, Rocco,' Nico introduces us. 'He runs the bar here. I look after *everything* else.'

'A pleasure, Clare,' Rocco welcomes me, also with a double cheek kiss, which stirs up the already fluttering butterflies in my stomach.

'Wow, good genes,' I say.

'Thanks,' the boys reply in unison, touching their hands to their trousers.

'So, now you've met everyone. And had a coffee,' Paola looks judgmentally at my barely touched cup of cappuccino, 'we get to work.'

Chapter 5

11 am

Paola sweeps behind the grand reception desk, an elegant setup with twin computer screens, with the villa name emblazoned across the front, and gestures for me to sit, pulling out a wheeled office chair with a flourish. I perch on the seat, but something feels off. It takes me a second to realise: there isn't a single keyboard in sight.

'How do we type?' I ask, looking side to side, then under the desk and at the credenza behind us.

'We don't. These are just for show,' she smiles, pointing to the screens. 'Makes us look modern, don't you think?'

'It would be more modern if we could use them,' I reply, disappointed that my Computing Concepts 101 paper, recently acquired from TAFE, will not be coming in handy.

'Pffft,' she dismisses me. Spinning on her chair, she slides open the credenza and extracts a small pile of faxes, placing them on the desk in front of me. Next, she opens a large, leatherbound diary and slides it towards me. 'For each tour arriving, your office will send us a fax,' Paola points to the faxes in case I'm not clear on what a fax looks like. 'Your job is to take each of the faxes and transfer the information to the correct date on the diary,' which she also points to. '*Allora*, the first tour arrives on Monday, so you turn to that date,' Paola explains, reaching for the faxes and pulling the top one off. 'On the page you write the tour code, which is, 'she squints behind her 'for show' glasses searching for the detail, 'FZ9727'.'

I carefully scribe FZ9727 at the top of the page next to the date.

'*Bene*!' Paola encourages as one would a child writing their name for the first time. 'Now you write the tour manager and the *autista*, I mean driver's names. In this case, it is Sharon

Green and Skipper. *Ma che cazzo*? Is that his real name?'

'No, it's his nickname. Most of the drivers have nicknames.' It's my turn to be the teacher. 'Usually, they get given them on a training trip because they've said something stupid or they crash into something. The name then sticks, and no one remembers what their real names are after a while.'

'Hmmfff,' Paola scoffs like it's the most stupid thing she's ever heard.

'They're a couple, Shaz and Skipper,' I expand. 'Usually, the office doesn't put couples together on a tour, so they are either really short-staffed or Shaz and Skipper are in the good books.'

'Good information. We give them a double room and save on the cleaning,' Paola states.

'On that, Paola. Does Maria clean all the rooms by herself? That's a lot on a Wednesday to clean and change all those rooms when one tour leaves and the other arrives.' I don't want to be ageist, but Maria looked well over 60.

'*Non*. Maria does the general cleaning around the villa. On a changeover day, her daughters will come in and do the rooms while Maria looks after their *bambine*.' Paola explains to my relief. '*Allora,* next, you write the total number of passengers, which in this case is 40,' she pauses for longer than is strictly necessary for me to write two numbers. 'Then the room breakdown list form. This time is 4 Doubles, 20 Females, 12 Males, and 2 staff. And you write if the staff are male/female, male/male or female/female. Is that possible female/female?'

'Technically yes,' I beam with feminist pride. 'We do have a couple of female drivers; they might work with a female tour manager.'

'Mamma mia!' she sighs. 'We write that so we know if they can share a room. Usually, we will try to give them a room each, but if we are busy, then boys might have to share, or girls, and in this case, if they are a couple, they can share.'

I look around the empty atrium and wonder when this busy time might be if it's not in July. I've yet to see an actual guest in the flesh, although Paola assures me there are some in-house.

'Next, you write the list of dietary requirements. Anna will check here so she knows how many omelettes to cook for the vegetarians,' she rolls her eyes. 'God did not make us to be vegetarians. We served melon wrapped with prosciutto to a vegetarian once, and they complained. *Per l'amor di Dio*, it's not like it's proper meat, just prosciutto.'

I appreciate the way Paola can take something that should be black or white and turn it into any shade of grey. In her world, cappuccino isn't really coffee, and prosciutto somehow qualifies as a vegetable. Her fluid relationship with the truth reminds me of Bill Clinton's infamous claim that he tried pot but didn't inhale. I mean, what did he do with it, insert it?

'*Finita*! For the first one, anyway,' Paola says, seemingly pleased with my ability to copy English words from one piece of paper to another. 'Now you do the next ones for the rest of July. Your office will send us details for August in a couple of weeks.'

While Paola writes figures in a ledger, which she's told me will be my next thing to learn, I work my way through the pile of faxes, noting down details and getting excited by some of the road crew names that I'll get to see again. At the sound of a motorini coming down the driveway, I pop my head, meerkat style, above the high counter to see who's coming.

A burly man without a helmet dwarfs the small bike; he brings it to a stop outside. I recognise him as one of the men who carried the tea chest the other day for Mario. Maybe even the one who put his mitt on my shoulder, although I was too taken aback to differentiate the two at the time. Rocco leaves the bar and goes out to meet the man who hands him a thick white envelope. After they exchange a few words, the man turns around and heads back up the driveway. Rocco comes inside. I duck my head down so as not to appear that I was watching.

Rocco approaches Paola and, without a word, hands her the envelope and walks back to the bar. Paola takes a stack of lira out of the envelope and proceeds to count it. As I continue to write surreptitiously, I watch her out of the corner of my eye. All of the notes appear to be of 100,000 denomination. Paola counts 10 and places them in a pile, repeating the process until she has 10 piles of a million lira.

'I will show you how to do this, but not today,' Paola tells me, picking up her pencil. 'All I'm doing for now is writing 1,000,000 received in the ledger next to the event that is booked in for Saturday.'

'Ohhh, what event is on?' I ask excitedly.

'A wedding,' she replies.

'I LOVE weddings. I hope I get to help,' I plead.

'It's cancelled,' Paola deadpans.

'What do you mean it's cancelled? You just said…'

'Pftttt,' Paola silences me. 'Keep writing the diary.' She collects up the piles of cash, replaces them in the envelope and slides it into the drawer next to her, turning a silver key to lock it, which she removes and drops into her handbag.

Chapter 6

Monday, July 7th

10 am

There's a buzz of anticipation in the air as Paola and I drink our regular morning coffee on the patio while we watch a shirtless Nico vacuum the pool. Well, Paola drinks her coffee. I raise the cup to my lips every so often, take a tiny sip, but a big breath in through my nose. Sniffing coffee seems to have become part of my anxiety-busting routine. It's like a breathing exercise, but one that smells good, and that I can do with someone without them even knowing I'm doing it. That and watching Nico's biceps bulge and relax as he pushes the vacuum around the pool are a great way to start the day.

'Do you think we are ready for the first tour?' Paola asks nervously.

'Of course,' I reassure her. 'Maria's daughters have made all the beds, and Maria has the place shining. Today is easy. They arrive, the tour manager will tell them their room numbers, and we will have the keys lined up on the counter for them to collect. Then they disappear. Later, Shaz will walk them down to Bussola Sud for dinner.'

'That's it?' Paola asks, surprised.

'Sure, until the problems start,' I laugh.

'The problems?'

'Someone loses their key, their passport, or they can't work the phone to call home. Someone is sick and needs a doctor, or a therapist, or both. There's always something. Especially by the time that they get this far into a tour. But don't worry, it won't be anything we can't handle.' I pat Paola reassuringly on the back.

4 pm

The ring from the reception desk phone echoes through the atrium.

Paola picks up the handset, '*Pronto*.' After a quick conversation, she says, 'That was Mario. The group have just left Moretti and Son's and is on their way.'

'Right.' I respond. I feel the cold creep of anxiety in my chest. I do a quick set of box breathing. I inhale for 4, hold for 4, exhale for 4, hold for 4 and repeat as I slowly look around the room. Room keys are lined up in order along the counter, ready for collection. Through the open bar doors, I can see that Rocco is filling trays of glasses with orange juice as a welcome drink, and Maria is scurrying around with a duster looking for any speck out of place.

'I make snacks for group.' Anna announces as she advances purposefully down the hall, carrying a tray of antipasto to go with the juice.

4.20 pm

A shiny green coach eases down the driveway. I walk outside to greet it. Something about it looks different, but I can't quite put my finger on it. Through the windscreen, I can see Shaz, microphone in one hand, the other waving furiously, issuing instructions to her flock as Skipper turns the coach in front of the villa, brings it to a stop and releases the door.

Shaz steps onto the pebbled driveway.

'Ciao.' She greets me with the traditional double kiss. 'They're ready for you.' She hands me the cordless microphone.

'You found it okay then?' I ask. They obviously did, so what has got Shaz rattled?

'Yeah, Mario's route notes were good, but fuck, those roads are narrow. Look,' she raises her eyes skyward. I follow her gaze.

The fly-eye passenger side mirror, which normally sits out from the side of the coach, is pushed flush against it, its glass smashed.

That's what looks different. And there it is, our first problem.

'Fuck,' I whisper, glancing at Skipper. He smiles and smacks his palm to his forehead.

'Not sure how he's so chill about it,' Shaz groans. 'I thought I was going to die. I'll go sort the rooming list. See you in there.'

'Hey, Skipper, rough day?' I greet one of my favourite drivers. You might be able to find a nicer guy, but I'm not sure how or where. As I step up into the aisle of the coach, Skipper exits to open the locker doors and prepare for luggage chaos. I raise the microphone to my mouth and flick the switch to on. 'Ciao and welcome to Villa delle Palme,' I smile broadly in what I hope is a welcoming way. 'We are excited to have you stay with us for the next couple of nights. Once you have your bag, you can take it into the reception area. Leave them there for a couple of minutes and go left in the bar, there Rocco has a drink for you and our lovely cook Anna has prepared a snack. When you are ready, see Shaz in reception and she will give you your room key. Breakfast in the morning is in the dining room at the back of the building, that's also where you'll find the pool if you want to cool off. You can get a pool towel from Nico's cabana next to the pool. Shaz will put your day sheet with all the times up somewhere in reception. If you have any questions, you can come and see me or Paola at reception any time until 8 pm. I hope you enjoy your stay.' I click the microphone off, place it back in its cradle and join Shaz in reception to help direct traffic. It's go time!

Chapter 7

Wednesday, July 9th

11 am

'Ready to do it all again?' I ask Paola after our morning coffee and perv at Nico.

'I guess,' she sighs. 'Do they always do that thing they call boat races until after midnight?'

'If they get the chance.' I laugh as Maria's stern-faced daughters come through the doors. Paola hands them a list of rooms that need to be cleaned and another list of rooms that need to be made up for the group of 25 passengers and 2 staff arriving this afternoon.

'Okay,' Paola says, all business now. 'I show you what we do after a tour leaves.'

'Yes, boss,' I salute, rolling my chair next to hers.

'*Prima*, you get an invoice sheet from this tray,' she reaches to a tiered tray system beside one of the screens, retrieving a piece of paper with some information pre-populated. 'Here,' she hands it to me. 'You put the date the tour left, so today. *Si.*

Next, you put the tour code.'

I switch my attention to the diary, flick the page back two days, then write FZ9727 in the appropriate box.

'Where it says total passengers, you write how many passengers,' she explains carefully.

I want to say that I'm pretty sure I could have worked all this out for myself, but I keep my mouth shut, adding a neat 40 to the page. '*Bene*, now in the item column you write, 40 @ two nights accommodation = 160,000 x 40 =,' she takes out a calculator and taps in numbers, 'six million, four hundred thousand lira. Underneath you write, '40 pax dinner @ 20,000 = eight hundred thousand lira. Okay?'

'All good, I passed grade 6 maths,' I say, the sarcasm lost in translation.

'*Bene*,' Paola continues, 'Next line you write, 2 x staff - F.O.C. I don't know what that means, but that's what Mario told me to do.'

'It means free of charge,' I explain. 'The staff get to stay for free when there are more than 20 passengers. Or at least that's the way the contracts are normally done.'

'Pffffft. Next line, we add it up. 6,400,000 + 800,000 is,' she turns back to the calculator.

'7,200,000,' I beat her to it.

'*Eccellente*! *Si*. Write it down. Now you sign, I sign, and you send it to Carlos on the fax machine. The Terrific Tours number is written beside the fax, see?' She asks as I glance at the machine on top of the credenza. 'While you do that, I'll put the information into the ledger.

I take the invoice to the fax machine and slide it onto the roller. Following the instructions on a yellowing scrap of paper taped beside it, I punch in the number and hit start. The machine whirs to life, letting out a series of loud beeps and electronic screeches before the familiar beep-beep signals that the other end is ready. As the paper feeds slowly into the machine, I glance over Paola's shoulder, watching as she writes in the ledger with quick, practised strokes.

'That doesn't look right, Paola. Our numbers were 6,400,000 + 800,000 for a total of 7,200,000. You've written 8,000,000 + 1,000,000 for a total of 9,000,000. That's 1.8 million out.' Surely she can't be that bad at maths?

'I know what I'm doing,' she snaps. Her shoulders tense, a subtle tell that my question has made her, what? Angry? Annoyed? Slamming the ledger shut, she puts it in the top drawer where the other day she placed the cash. She slams the drawer shut, locks it, and says, 'I'm going to take my lunch now. I'll be back before the next tour arrives.'

While the Wallan Wild Dogs bullying gave me ongoing anxiety, one upside of it is that it made me become very aware of other people and their moods. I had to, to survive. Wallan Primary School was a small and generally happy place for me in grades 1-5, but at the start of grade 6, Calista Nelson arrived from out of town. She'd come from the city, and she was cool. She had fashionable clothes bought from a shop, not sewn by her mum, and she had the latest chopper bike, which she rode to school every day.

Almost immediately, she attracted all the other grade 6 girls into her orbit, except me. For some reason, Callista Nelson didn't like me, and she made sure all the other girls in the year, whom I'd previously played with, felt the same way.

'Hey, plain Jane Brown,' she'd shouted at me within the first week of the term. When I corrected and said my name was Clare, she retorted, 'Only 'cause your parents named you before they saw you.' She laughed and looked at each girl in turn to make sure they were laughing too. They made the next three years hell. Being in class was tolerable as the teacher would shut down any shenanigans, but morning tea and lunch, I was on my own and fair game. Usually, I sat by myself with my back against a big tree that gave a good view of the yard. There, I knew I was protected from behind. I scanned the playground looking for any change in the girls' behaviour that would indicate they were heading towards me, to give me time to escape. I ponder what Paola's sudden change in voice tone could mean as I stare vacantly at the high atrium ceiling.

Friday, July 11th

11 am

'Well, that's our first week done, Paola,' I smile at my colleague as we take our places behind the desk.

The vibe over our regular morning coffee was a little frosty yesterday, but it was much better today, and to make it improve it further, Nico decided to clean the pool while he was swimming in it. While the tiniest budgie smugglers I've ever seen on a man covered most of his bum, the rest of his body glistened beautifully in the water as he paddled about pushing the vacuum.

'Yes. Now, do you remember how to make the invoice?' She asks.

'Sure do,' I reply confidently, pulling a template from the tray.

'Great, you do that, then I'll do the ledger. Oh, and Mario wants you to pop down and see him after lunch,' she says.

'Sure, a ride into town will be nice,' I smile, wondering why on earth Mario wants to see me. After I complete the invoice calculations for 25 passengers, I read the numbers out to Paola, who notes them down on a scrap of paper. As the fax machine beeps and screeches, I quietly peer over Paola's shoulder as she writes in the journal. Again, she inflates the numbers by about 20%. This time, I say nothing.

Chapter 8

My long blonde locks below the orange helmet fly out behind me as I head downhill. The piazza is busy as I park the tangerine dream with the other mopeds, cross the road and enter Moretti and Sons.

'Clare,' Mario greets me warmly. 'Come to my office. We'll have coffee and chat.'

I can't bring myself to tell him that I really don't want or need coffee. Taking a few sips each morning while I do my inhaling is enough for me, but I don't want to appear rude. As soon as we sit down on opposite sides of Mario's desk, a woman places a small cup of espresso in front of each of us. '*Allora*, how has the first week been?'

'Good,' I smile. 'The clients love the villa, so does the road crew.'

'*Molto bene*,' he nods, pleased. 'And my staff?'

'Also good. Maria keeps the place spick and span. Anna's breakfasts and dinners are delicious, Rocco keeps everyone entertained in the bar and the drinks flowing, and Nico, it's a pleasure to watch his work in the pool.' I hope Mario doesn't pick up on my unintentional double entendre.

'*Bene, bene*. And Paola?' he asks.

'Paola is great,' I reply.

'You have questions?' he asks, before downing his espresso in one gulp.

'A couple,' I pause, unsure of how to phrase them. 'Is it common that a wedding would be booked, paid for in cash and then cancelled?'

Something darkens behind Mario's eyes, '*Si*, here it is common. Next question?'

'I was just wondering why the numbers in the ledger are more than the numbers on the invoices to Terrific Tours, shouldn't they match?'

The darkness in Mario's eyes intensifies, 'I will talk to Paola,' he replies.

'I hope I haven't gotten her into trouble?' I'm worried I've poked my nose into something I shouldn't have.

'Of course not, Clare. Now you take care riding that motorini back up to the villa, won't you?' He says in a tone of voice that sends a small shiver up my spine.

Saturday, July 12th - 3 am

I wake with a start from a dream where I've locked myself in a toilet cubicle at Wallan Primary School, and the Wild Dogs are trying to get in to me. The door rattles as they shake it, the lock barely holding out. With a final push, the cubicle door flies inwards, slamming against the cubicle wall. I wake myself before they get to me, blood racing, beads of sweat on my forehead. Outside, I hear what sounds like plastic wheels on concrete. Hopping down from my high bed, I walk to the small living area and peer out the small window. The lights on the villa patio cast just enough light for me to make out a burly man walking around the side of the pool, heading towards the lemoniaia side of the building. Behind him, he drags a large suitcase. Whatever's in it, it looks to be heavy.

10 am

'Your coffee.' Anna places two steaming mugs of cappuccino on the table and returns to the kitchen.

Anna is chatty as ever.

I take the tiniest of sips, wanting to save my small sips and my pretend sips for when Paola joins me, and instead do some deep inhales. Although after a broken sleep last night, some caffeine might be helpful.

'Nico,' I call out, torn as I want to ask him a question, but I don't want him to stop the rhythmic underwater hip thrusting he's doing as he pushes the pool vacuum.

'*Si*,' he replies.

'Have you seen Paola this morning?' I shout.

'No.' His answer comes thankfully without him breaking his stride or thrust.

With the coffee now cold, I head down the stairs to the stable.

'Going to join me in the pool?' Nico winks.

'Tempting,' I smile, and I'm not lying, 'but no, not yet.'

Passing my door, I head to Paola's, rapping on it gently.

'Paola, are you there?' When there's no response, I rap louder and louder, eventually banging the door with my fist.

Still no response.

Where the hell is she?

Maybe she usually gets the weekends off, and no one told me?

Maybe she got lucky last night somewhere, and she'll do a walk of shame home sometime today. Yes, that's probably it. I hope I'm around to see her skulking back in. Smiling at the thought, I head inside to see if any new tour faxes have arrived overnight.

As I approach the reception desk, I catch sight of the top of a head of dark hair. For a moment, I think it's Paola, but then I spot the sun-kissed streaks threading through the dark, and the head lifts.

Not Paola.

A man.

A devastatingly handsome man.

He looks to be around my age, with artfully tousled hair swept back in a perfect wave, the kind of effortless style that probably takes effort. A neatly trimmed beard traces the sharp lines of his jaw, with a hint of stubble under his bottom lip and a dark moustache drawing my gaze, unhelpfully, to a mouth that looks far too kissable for a stranger. His eyebrows, thick and dark, frame eyes so green they could start traffic. Or hearts. Definitely hearts. Subconsciously, I gently rub my tattoo. As I do, I can feel my pulse hammering against the skin. He's got my heart going.

'Who are YOU?' Is what falls a little aggressively out of my mouth.

'Ciao,' he says, rising with an easy smile as he strides toward me, all warmth and quiet confidence.

He wears a faded denim shirt, the sleeves casually rolled to just below his elbows, revealing forearms that are tanned, muscular, and entirely distracting. A chunky, high-end watch, maybe a TAG, rests on his left wrist, gleaming subtly with understated wealth. His oatmeal-hued chinos fit like they were tailored just for him, striking the perfect balance between effortless and refined. On his feet, classic tan leather boat shoes complete the look, expensive, but worn in, like he's not trying too hard.

Of course, he isn't.

He doesn't have to.

His aftershave smells like the landscape, earthy but fresh with notes of citrus.

'I'm Luca.' He leans down, kissing each cheek slowly. Each kiss grazes a corner of my mouth. It takes every ounce of my self-control not to either turn my head and make it a proper kiss or poke my tongue out a little so it can feel his lips. 'And you must be Clare?'

And Clare is in trouble, I think, before replying, 'yes'.

'*Grande*. Join me, Clare.' Luca moves back behind the desk. 'I was just reviewing the faxes.

'Why?' I stammer. 'Where's Paola?' A bolt of anxiety hits hard. As I lower myself onto my chair, I do a quick set of box breaths to try and get rid of it.

'My father has replaced Paola with me,' he smiles.

'You're Mario's son?' Now he says it, I can see the resemblance. And why wouldn't he be? Everyone else here is related. 'But where's Paola? She didn't even say goodbye.'

'Don't worry, Clare, it's not like the Godfather, we didn't shoot her,' he laughs heartily at what I hope is a joke. 'She went home to Naples early this morning. I'm going to be your new neighbour and colleague.'

I laugh nervously, my mind racing. 'How's your maths, Luca? Better than Paola's,' I ask, fishing for a reaction.

'You don't need to worry about my maths,' Luca says smoothly.

His expression doesn't flicker. He's cool, unreadable. This man could be a challenge.

Chapter 9

Midday

'Zia Anna,' Luca calls to his Aunt.

'Si,' her reply echoes down the hall.

'Per favore, can you prepare lunch for Clare and me to take on the patio?'

'Si,' she grunts.

'Grazie, zia!' He calls back. 'Isn't she the sweetest thing?' He asks as he pushes himself back from the desk.

'Sweet enough to give you a stomach ulcer,' I smile, hoping it masks my sarcasm.

He gives me a questioning look but doesn't delve.

'Andiamo.' Luca places a hand on the small of my back to steer me away from the desk. I'm fully capable of walking in a straight line, but hey, who am I to argue with a handsome man and a little unnecessary touching? At that moment, a burly man on a motorini pulls up. 'You go ahead,' Luca says, letting his hand slide off my back, brushing the top of my bum in the process. I could be offended, but then he might not do it again.

'It's okay, I can wait,' I smile, challenging him.

'Fine,' he replies, going outside to meet the man. Luca places himself between me and the motorini so I can't see what is happening, and I certainly can't understand what is being said. He turns back towards me as the motorini powers back down the driveway. It could be my imagination, but I think the bulge in his chinos is more pronounced than before.

I vow to myself to pay extra special attention to Luca's pants in the future. A mission I'm happy to accept.

'*Grazie, zia* Anna,' Luca smiles warmly at his Aunt as she places a large platter in front of us.

She returns with two side plates and two large wine glasses. On her third trip, she places an uncorked bottle of wine.

'*Buon appetito*,' Anna says before scurrying back into the kitchen.

As Luca pours white wine into our glasses, I take a slice of bread, a slice of creamy mozzarella, some grilled zucchini and a slice of prosciutto from the platter and place them on my plate.

'Is it vegetarian prosciutto?' I joke, thinking of Paola.

'Um,' Luca starts, unsure of how to answer this ridiculous question.

'It's a joke,' I explain.

'Oh, ha! So, Clare, tell me about yourself.' Luca sucks an olive between his lips and rolls it around his mouth before chewing.

I'm momentarily entranced watching his mouth move, his expression behind his mirrored glasses impossible to read. I'm grateful for my own dark sunglasses, which hopefully disguise the fact that I'm staring.

'There's not much to tell. I'm originally from a small town just outside Melbourne. I went to high school in Melbourne, then moved to Carlton to go flatting with my best friends Nicky and Toni.' I pause to take a sip of wine.

Luca fills the momentary silence. 'Did you like school?'

'I didn't mind high school, that's where I met Nicky and Toni. It was a big city school with lots of kids, and for the most part, everyone just got on with what they were into and let everyone else do their thing. Primary school was a different story. I went to a small country school where a group of girls made my life hell for three years.' I take another long sip of wine to stop any anxiety in its tracks.

'Oh, Clare,' he says, placing his hand on top of mine, giving it a quick, reassuring squeeze, 'that sounds awful.'

'After a few years in Carlton,' I say, moving the conversation away from my trauma as quickly as I can, 'Nicky, Toni, and I had saved up some money, so we booked on a Terrific Tours tour of Europe. Afterwards, I went home, decided I wanted to work in Europe, applied for a visa and a job with Terrific Tours and got both. I started working for the company in 1995. And here I am now. What about you, Luca? Tell me your life story.' I put the entire slice of prosciutto in my mouth, savouring its saltiness.

'I really don't have much to tell,' he smiles. 'I was born in Sorrento, went to school in Sorrento, went to university up the road in Naples, now I work for my father.'

'No childhood trauma you're dying to unpack? Embarrassing hobbies? Worst-ever gifts from your girlfriend you'd like to bitch about?' I cast the line and take a drink of wine while I wait for a bite.

'Ha! My mother used to cut my hair until I was about 10, and in every childhood photo, I look like I'm wearing a bowl on my head. My hobby is rebuilding cars. I've just finished a 1986 Alfa Romeo Spider. It's black as night and sexy as hell.' He beams with pride. 'Maybe I can take you for a drive tomorrow?'

'Sounds fun,' I reply.

'And no, I don't have a girlfriend.' He lifts his glass and takes a slow sip of wine, the words lingering in the air between us, rich with possibility.

Sunday - 3 pm

'Are you ready?' Luca asks.

He's sitting behind the wheel of the sports car he rebuilt from a write-off, and looking proud as punch with it. He's right, it is sexy as hell. They both are. The car is sleek and timeless, and exudes a raw, effortless sexiness, like a midnight whisper that promises adventure with every curve and purr of its engine. Luca has on a casual white t-shirt, his sunglasses are on his head, pushing his hair out of his face. His green eyes sparkle with joy.

'Ready,' I smile, skipping down the villa steps in my white sandshoes. It's only when I slide into the low passenger seat that I realise we are wearing almost identical outfits. White t-shirts, cream chinos and white shoes. He clocks it at the same time. We stare at each other for a moment, 'Shall I change?' I ask, laughing.

'No, let's roll with it,' he laughs. 'Ready for a ride?'

'Let's not call it a mindless joyride. Let's call it an escape!' I quote Thelma, or was it Louise, as I lower my glasses over my eyes and pull a sunhat out of my tote bag, placing it firmly on my head.

The first leg of the drive is calm enough as we head toward Sorrento, until Luca takes a left at the end of Via Pasano instead of a right. Suddenly, we're off the familiar map. The road narrows, curling around hills and weaving through sleepy clusters of houses. Luca handles the Alfa like he was born behind the wheel, effortlessly dodging oncoming Vespas and grazing stone walls with the precision of a man who's done this a hundred times before. After a while, I stop closing my eyes at every turn, relax and start to enjoy the views of lemon groves and the glittering sea below.

'We'll take the coastal route,' Luca says, as if he's reading my mind.

'Coastal route to where?' I ask.

'You'll see,' he replies cryptically.

After thirty minutes of sea-scented wind in my hair and roads that twist tighter with every turn, we glide through the quiet village of Termini. When the lane shrinks to something barely wider than a Vespa, Luca pulls over beside an open patch of sun-drenched grass and kills the engine.

'We're here,' he says, flashing a grin. Then, with all the flourish of an old-school movie star, he vaults over his car door, rounds the bonnet, and opens mine with a gallant bow.

'Wow.' That's all I can say as I look past the meadow down to the sea and across the Isle of Capri. While I'm gazing, Luca extracts from the boot a picnic blanket, a bottle and two glasses.

Flapping the blanket out dramatically onto the grass, he suggests that I sit.

'This is beautiful, Luca.'

'*Si*,' he says, popping the cork on a bottle of prosecco and filling two plastic flutes. '*Saluti*,' he says, touching the rim of his glass to mine.

'*Saluti*,' I respond, taking a sip.

'Your car is beautiful, Luca. You've done a great job.'

I'm not usually a car person. At home, I have a green Mazda 323 made sometime in the 80s, garaged at Mum and Dad's. As long as it runs, I'm happy, and I don't care what it looks like. But there is something alluring about Luca's sleek black sports car with the tan leather interior.

'*Grazie*,' he replies modestly. 'My uncle Enzo, Rocco's father, got the wreck for me. He runs a car dealership in town that has a workshop attached, so I could work on it there.'

'That's handy, and probably free too. Using your large family wisely.' I smile.

'There's always a price to pay with my family,' Luca says cryptically.

He downs the last of his prosecco and stands. 'Shall we go? I'll take you into town and teach you how to eat like an Italian.'

Chapter 10

Safely back in Sorrento, Luca parks in Piazza Torquato Tasso. Once again, he opens my door for me, and we stroll in comfortable silence. Now that we are around other people, I'm conscious of our almost identical outfits. It's giving me cult, but hopefully we are giving off fashion.

'Oh, this one looks nice,' I suggest as we pass a small trattoria. 'It's busy, so it must be good.'

'No,' he replies without looking, 'We cannot go there.'

'What do you mean, cannot?' I challenge. 'It looks nice. I'd like to try it.'

'No,' he repeats firmly. 'This is owned by a rival family. It is forbidden for me. You try it by yourself if you want. Just make sure Mario doesn't find out.'

'What's Mario going to do, leave a horse head in my bed?' I try to make a joke.

'It's the way it is, Clare. We go to a restaurant owned by my family.' He walks on, leaving me in his wake to follow, but with so many questions. Why are families rivals? Doesn't it get boring only being able to go to places your family owns? Mind you, the family does seem massive; maybe that provides plenty of opportunities. I decide to save all of these questions for another day and enjoy a meal with my new co-worker/frie nd/clothing twin.

Monday 14th July - 9 am

As I finish fixing my face for the day with a light brush of lip gloss, there's a rattle of a door handle, followed by a loud knock on the adjoining room door. I unlock the door and open it.

'Why is it locked?' Luca asks without greeting.

'Good morning to you too,' I snap. 'It's locked for privacy. My privacy obviously.'

'In my family, we don't lock doors. And we don't have privacy,' Luca beams. 'I thought we could go for a walk, get the morning started with some exercise?' He's dressed in activewear and ready to go. I, on the other hand, am dressed already for work in a long, flowy skirt and a blouse.

'Great! I love walking,' I respond enthusiastically. 'Just give me a minute to change.'

Luca plonks himself on my small couch like he owns the place, which I guess he kind of does, as I duck into my bedroom and change into a pair of Lycra shorts, a sports bralet and put socks and trainers on my feet. I tug a cap onto my head to protect my face from the sun.

'Let's go,' I say, stepping into the lounge where Luca waits.

He pauses, his gaze sliding slowly from my shoes upward, like a caress made of fire. Back home, I wear this to the gym without a second thought, but the way Luca's eyes linger, I suddenly feel like I've shown up in lingerie.

'Is this okay?' I ask nervously, not wanting to offend.

'*Si, bellissimo,*' he tears his gaze away. '*Andiamo.*'

Chapter 10

It feels good to stretch out into a brisk walk, my long, toned legs practically sighing with relief at being put to proper use again. After an hour, my skin glows with a slick sheen of sweat, breath coming in short, shallow bursts as we make our way back to the stables.

'That was a great way to start the day, thank you, Luca,' I say as I pause to sit on a deck chair and remove my shoes and socks.

'Always good to work up a sweat before breakfast. Not my favourite way, but still a good one,' he winks.

Suddenly, it's not just the workout that has me overheated. His innuendo sparks a flush that's creeping up my neck, and the last thing I want is for him to know the effect he has on me. Without a word, I rise and slip into the pool with a clean, elegant dive, leaving barely a ripple behind. When my head rises back above the water, he's gone.

11 am

Back in my skirt, blouse and a pair of leather sandals, I join Luca behind the reception desk.

'Ready for your first tour arrival day?' I ask.

'*Si*, born ready,' he smiles.

'I've got a few more tours to note in the diary and I have to fax my weekly report to Carlos,' I explain.

'*Si*, and I have stuff to do too,' he says confidently, but his face belies that he's not really sure what that stuff is. 'But first, I go to the *il bagno*.' He heads towards the bathrooms off the hallway.

The crunch of gravel and the whirring buzz of a motorini announce an arrival. Moments after it sputters to a stop, heavy footsteps echo. One of the burly men fills the doorway, scans the room, then strides toward the desk.

'*Dov'è Luca?*' he asks in a deep timbre.

The book of Italian phrases I've been studying each night pays off. At least, I understand him. Replying in a full sentence isn't possible.

'Bagno,' I respond, pointing towards the gents.

'*Si*,' he grunts, looking impatiently at his watch.

'Can I help?' I offer, pointing to myself.

He glances at his watch again, '*Si*,' he grunts again, reaching inside his leather jacket and retrieving a thick white envelope. 'You give Luca,' he commands in broken English. 'Tell her for, ah, fiesta, how say in English? Ah, party. Saturday.' He hands it to me reluctantly, returns to his motorini and speeds back down the driveway.

'Someone came to see you when you were in the *bagno*, Luca,' I tell him when he returns. 'One of Mario's henchmen.'

'Not henchmen, Clare, probably security,' he tries to explain.

'Okay, whatever. He said to give this to you.' I hand him the thick envelope.

'*Bene, si*, this is for the birthday party booked on Saturday night,' he explains.

He reaches into his pocket, retrieves a key and opens the top drawer where the ledger now stays. He pulls it out, opens it as far away from me as he possibly can, scribbles information down before returning it and the envelope to the drawer, locking it and pocketing the key.

I focus on the couple of faxes I have with new tour information. Before I copy the information onto the correct page, I surreptitiously glance at the page for Saturday night. On it is written in ink, 50th birthday party - 100 guests. Next to it in pencil it says, cancelled. After entering the tour details, I start on my weekly report.

Chapter 10

Weekly Report - Villa delle Palme

The first week for Terrific Tours at Villa delle Palme has gone well overall.

Arrivals: Both tours have arrived within the expected time frame

Breakfast: They have been good. A suitable mix of cereals, fruits and juices. Toast is able to be made, and cook Anna does a big tray of scrambled eggs for the hot item.

Dinner: Excellent. Anna cooks spaghetti bolognese and serves it with green salad and crusty bread, and loads of grated parmesan.

Bar: Barman Rocco makes sure everyone is having a good time and keeps shots of sambuca flowing. No complaints about noise. Having no close neighbours helps.

Cleaning: Maria and her daughters do a great job. The villa is always spotless. Nico ensures that the pool and grounds are tidy.

Reception: There was an unexplained sudden change in the receptionist.

Overall, I'm happy with how things have gone this week.

Anything needed: Can you please send some Vegemite with the next tour leaving London? I'm craving it.

Kind regards

Clare

10 pm

I'm just drifting off to sleep when the shrill ring of a phone cuts through the quiet. It's coming from Luca's room. The ringing stops, followed by the low murmur of his voice.

'Pronto... Ciao, Papà... Sì... Sì... La sto tenendo d'occhio...'

His tone sharpens, rising with every word.

'Te l'ho detto di sì. SÌ! PAPA!'

A long pause. Then, tightly clipped:

'Buona notte.'

The phone slams into its cradle, the sharp clack slicing through the silence like a slap.

Chapter 11

Wednesday, 8 pm

'Is every Wednesday like that?' Luca asks.

It's been non-stop, one group departing, another arriving. Finally, the arriving group has left for dinner at a different restaurant tonight, as Bussola Sud is closed for repairs. With no dinner to cook, Anna is off tonight, Nico has finished for the day and gone home, Maria's daughters have been and gone, and Rocco won't start until 10 pm, just in time for the group to start trickling back from their dinner looking for more alcohol. As usual, there are no other guests.

For now, the Villa is ours.

'Pretty much, yes,' I sigh, taking a deep breath of still night air. 'Let's enjoy the serenity.

'Mamma mia!' He exclaims. 'Have you eaten?'

'Not since lunch.' My stomach rumbles on cue to remind me that an apple and a cookie do not a lunch make.

'Un momento,' Luca says, disappearing into the kitchen. He returns moments later with a bottle of wine under one arm, two glasses in his hand. Balancing on his other hand is a platter.

'Help me please,' he requests, moving the platter to within reach. I take it from him and place it on the table. On it is a knife, a baguette, a round of some kind of soft cheese, a couple of tomatoes, a handful of grapes, some artichoke hearts and some kind of cured meat. 'A pauper's dinner. But it's food.'

'It's perfect. Thanks, Luca.'

Luca uncorks the red wine, pouring generously into each glass. I slice the tomatoes and cut the cheese into wedges. Luca tears the bread apart with his hands, passing me a chunk. I place a triangle of cheese, a slice of meat and tomato and some artichoke hearts in the middle and fold the edges of the piece of baguette around it to make a makeshift sandwich.

'Compliments to the chef,' I say after my first bite.

We eat and sip wine in comfortable silence, watching the sky turn pink, then orange, then black. The only light comes behind us from the atrium at the end of the hall, and above, the full moon, and a sky scattered with stars. When the bottle is empty and the platter bare, Luca turns to me. 'Swim?'

'How long have we got till the clients come back?' I ask.

Luca turns his wrist, and illuminated dots light up on his watch.

'It's 8.45 - so we've got at least 45 minutes. Race you,' he challenges. We jostle for position down the stairs, laughing before taking off towards our respective doors. Of course, he wins. His legs are longer and stronger, and as soon as I start running, I realise I've drunk more wine than I should, and I feel a little giddy and unsteady on my feet.

'I let you win,' I say as I open my door and duck in to get changed.

Luca is already in the pool when I step out of my room. My

white bikini catches the moonlight, luminous against my skin. His eyes lock onto me, tracking my every move.

'Over here,' he calls, his voice low and warm.

I follow the sound, guided by him and the glimmer of the water, until the roughness of the path gives way to smooth tile. I sink slowly to the edge of the pool, dipping my legs into the cool, inviting water. He appears in front of me, his hand reaching out like an invitation. I place mine in his, and as I slip into the water, our fingers intertwine. He draws me gently into a slow, playful turn, the world blurring around us. Then he eases me to a stop, guiding me until my feet find the bottom, releasing my hands. My hair floats around me like a halo, and for a moment, it feels like we're the only two people in the universe.

'Do you mind working here, Luca?' I ask.

'Mind?' He asks, 'I'm not sure in English exactly what this means. It is my duty. My father commands it, so I do it.'

'If you could do anything in the world, what would it be?' We drift around each other in slow circles, a moonlit dance beneath the water's surface. The silver light glimmers just enough for me to take him in: broad, bare shoulders rising above the pool, and beneath the surface, the sculpted lines of his abdomen, framed by a trace of dark chest hair and the curve of strong, defined pecs.

'I would rebuild cars,' he says dreamily.

'A panelbeater?' I ask.

'*Si.* I would beat panels and make beautiful cars.' His teeth catch the moonlight when he smiles, in the same way my bikini does.

I wonder how it would feel to kiss those lips, to taste the softness beneath that perfectly trimmed beard against my face, or lower, where want gathers like a storm. Slowly, almost imperceptibly, the circle we've been tracing begins to tighten. My chest hovers mere millimetres from his. Then I feel his hands, warm and sure, settle on my hips, right where the ties of my bikini rest. Our faces inch closer, breath mingling in the moonlit stillness.

My bikini top brushes against his chest, just the faintest touch, yet it sparks an almost unbearable friction.

'CLARE. CLARE!'

The urgent shout slices through the night like a siren, jolting us apart in an instant. The air between us snaps back to reality just as tour manager, Stacey, strides onto the patio, her voice tight with urgency.

'There you are,' she says, breathless. 'Clare, we've got a situation.'

...

'What's wrong?' I ask Stacey. Luca and I are both dressed, but our hair is still dripping as we meet Stacey in the atrium. In the corner of the room, two girls sob, comforting each other.

'A couple of things, but most urgently, two of my girls,' she says at a normal volume, then whispers, 'those two dumbasses over there.' Back to normal volume, 'Had their passports stolen at the bar.' Whispering, 'what kind of idiots take their passports to a pub for fucks sake.'

'That's terrible news,' I say. With my back to the girls, I roll my eyes, quietly showing Stacey I'm on her side, understanding that her relaxing night has just been hijacked by a drama she never asked for.

'I can sort this,' Luca says confidently.

'How? Those passports will be long gone by now. Luca, can you find out for me when a bus goes from here to Rome? They'll need to get to the embassy, get new passports, then maybe they can fly to Corfu and meet us there.' Stacey is in full problem-solving mode.

'I told you, I can sort this,' Luca says. He walks towards the girls, squats down and places each of his hands on one of their knees. They turn from sobbing to entranced as this handsome Italian man with dripping wet hair talks to them gently. As my heart slowly melts, he says, 'Don't worry. This will be okay. I will take care of it for you. Now go, have a drink, enjoy yourself.' He shouts over the music, 'ROCCO, GET THESE GIRLS WHATEVER THEY WANT TO DRINK, ON ME.' He strides confidently over the reception desk, picks up the telephone and dials. 'Papà, sono Luca.'

While he's talking to his father, Stacey says, 'Who the fuck does he think he is? How is the receptionist going to get back two stolen passports?'

'I'm not sure, Stacey, but I think there's more going on here than meets the eye. I don't know what it all is, but I trust Luca. Let's see what he can do. If it's nothing, then I'll help the girls get to Rome the day you leave for Brindisi. How does that sound?' For now, Stacey's other problem is forgotten.

Thursday - 4 pm

'I made you a baby coffee,' Luca says with a grin, setting a cappuccino on the desk in front of me.

'You made it? Or did Anna, and you're just the pretty delivery boy?' I tease, raising an eyebrow.

He laughs, rich and unguarded, and it sends a little spark through me. 'You know me too well already. Dangerous.'

'You know I don't drink coffee, let alone in the afternoon. I look like I need it?' I smile.

'Well, when I left the bar at midnight, you were throwing back sambuca shots like they were candy and dragging people onto the dancefloor. So yeah, I figured a little caffeine might be helpful.'

'I had to help Stacey get over her stress,' I laugh. 'And nearly kill myself in the process.'

A motorini pulls to a stop outside the villa, and a burly man appears at the door. It seems I've stopped getting a jump scare every time this happens, or maybe the hangover is dulling my reactions. The burly man approaches Luca. Without a word from inside one side of his leather jacket, he pulls out the usual, thick, white envelope and hands it to Luca. He reaches into the other side of his jacket. Like a magician, he pulls out two Australian passports and presents them to me.

'Oh. My. God.' I stammer. '*Grazie! Grazie mille*!' The burly man nods his head, turns and goes back the way he came. 'You did it, Luca!' I leap from my chair, throw my arms around his neck, and press a lingering kiss to his cheek, longer than necessary, warm against his skin. Slowly, deliberately, he turns his head. My lips glide along his stubbled jaw as he moves, until they find his, waiting, wanting, and the kiss deepens, inevitable.

'Get a room,' Stacey's driver, Nails, says as he saunters through the atrium.

The moment is broken, we pull apart. 'I'm sorry,' I stammer. 'So unprofessional to be doing that in reception.'

'You're right,' he agrees. My heart sinks for a moment, then he says, 'We will do it somewhere more private next time.'

5.30 pm

'Ta da.' I present Stacey with two passports like a magician revealing their trick.

'That's amazing, thanks,' she says. Her response is a little underwhelming. 'Can you hold them for a minute, I…' She turns on her heels and sprints to the bathroom.

'What's up with her?' Luca asks.

I shrug.

Some time later, Stacey exits the bathroom and approaches the desk again.

'With all the drama of the passports, I didn't tell you about my other problem last night,' she says.

'Are you okay?' I ask, worried. Stacey's skin is a weird colour and small beads of sweat line her forehead.

'Not really,' she confirms. 'You know who we got sent to that other restaurant last night? Well, about ¾ of the group ordered the chicken. They were all eating happily until one girl, who's really paranoid about eating undercooked meat, sliced all the way through the chicken and opened it up. Guess what she found?'

'I'm not sure I want to know,' I reply.

'I definitely don't,' Luca says.

'Maggots!'

I gag involuntarily. 'No!'

'Yes. Then the rest of the people eating the chicken dissected theirs as well. All of them had maggots.' Stacey runs to the bathroom again.

'That's not good,' Luca says, stating the obvious.

Not many of Stacey's group, or Stacey turned up for Anna's dinner, much to Anna's annoyance, and the bar stayed eerily quiet; the most came from the nearly constant flushing of toilets around the villa.

Friday - 9.30 am

'I hope Maria's daughters have strong stomachs,' I say to Luca,

15 minutes after Stacey, Nails, and their group rolled out of the villa gates, 45 minutes after they were supposed to depart.

'I would not want to be on that bus today. And having to drive all the way to Brindisi, *mamma mia*!' Luca holds his nose and laughs.

We take our places behind the desk, I check the fax machine, and Luca takes a key from his pants pocket and unlocks the secret drawer.

'Oh merda,' he swears.

'What?' I ask, instantly worried, immediately on high alert.

Luca pulls something out of the drawer and holds it up for me. 'Stacey's passport. In all the chaos of sick passengers, she must have forgotten it.'

'Fuck.'

'*Si, Fanculo*.'

'She's supposed to be leaving Italy today. She's not going to be able to do that without her passport. Think, Luca. What can we do?' I ask.

'I can catch the bus,' he says confidently. 'I will take the spider for a spin and chase that bus down,' he smiles at the prospect. 'I will be back soon.'

With that, he places the passport in his pocket and races out the door. In his haste, he forgets to lock the top drawer.

Chapter 12

Saturday

10 am

I knock twice gently on the adjoining door, 'Luca?'

'Entrare,' comes a sleepy reply.

I unlock my side of the adjoining door, turn the handle and push. Of course, he doesn't have his side locked; Luca doesn't do privacy. After Thursday's kiss, I tried to not be within kissing range of him yesterday. Every time he came within what I deemed kissing range, I moved away and found something urgent to do. It helped that he was gone for an hour or so chasing a bus at speed on the autostrada. At 6 pm, I feigned a headache and escaped to my room, and locked all my doors to be alone with my thoughts.

I shouldn't have let Luca kiss me.

Or did I kiss him?

I'm still not 100% sure. Either way, he's the son of my boss. Fuck this up, and I could get fired, or worse, if Mario finds out.

I tiptoe through his small lounge, the hush of morning

wrapping around me. His bedroom door is ajar. I pause in the doorway, breath catching. Soft light spills through the narrow window, casting a golden glow across the bed. A tangle of white sheets clings low on his hips, barely veiling the evidence of his morning arousal. I force my gaze upward, slowly tracing the lines of his torso, the rise and fall of sculpted abs, the smooth dip of his chest. His arms are folded behind his head, biceps flexed, dark underarm hair exposed, effortlessly masculine. His face is turned toward me, still and serene in sleep, lips parted, eyes closed. Beautiful. Unaware. Tempting.

For fucks sake, Clare, I admonish myself. 'Luca?'

'*Ciao bella*,' he replies, prising his eyes apart. 'What's up?'

'Just letting you know I'm heading into Sorrento for most of the day. I'll see you later.' I turn to leave.

Luca bolts upright, suddenly wide awake. The sheet slips lower, revealing the top of his pubic hair. I glance away, flushed with embarrassment. He catches my reaction, hastily pulls the sheet up, then glances down and realises why.

Now we're both mortified.

'I'll come with you. Wait for me,' he says, about to leap out of bed.

'No, Luca, I want to go by myself. I'll be back this afternoon.'

'Clare, I'm coming,' he asserts.

Anger flares in me.

'Luca, I'm going alone. And since you've clearly got a situation to handle,' I gesture pointedly at the tented sheet, 'I don't think there's much you can do to stop me.' I spin on my heel and storm out, slamming the door behind me for emphasis.

I use extra accelerator on my motorini as I head down the hill to Sorrento, letting the wind try to blow away my anger. I don't need a man to help me buy tampons for fucks sake. Maybe it's coming to the end of my period that has made me so angry? I'm also tired of only having the food available in the kitchen. I want to buy some snacks, maybe have a picnic for one by the pool tonight. Surely Luca is allowed to have his own life on a Saturday night and has friends to go out with or something. A little alone time will do me good. I park my motorini in its usual spot, sling my tote bag over my shoulder and head off in search of a supermarket.

One of my favourite things to do in a foreign country is browse the aisles of a supermarket, and today I take them extra slowly. I pick up a couple of pieces of fresh fruit from the produce section before heading off in search of tampons, chocolate and wine. Perfect period first aid. As I'm deliberating between Tampax and Carefree, I get a sense that I'm being watched.

I flick my head to the left.

A weasely man in a black t-shirt and jeans quickly turns his face to the shelves, then scurries away. He's probably buying tampons for his girlfriend, and he's embarrassed I looked at him, I think, as I pull a box of Tampax from the shelf and toss it in my basket. After a block of dark chocolate joins them, I linger in the wine aisle, white or red? As I pull a bottle of red off a centre aisle display, in the gap where it was, through the display, I see the same weasly man.

I jump back in fright.

He picks up a bottle of wine from the same display and walks casually away.

Anxiety sits at the base of my throat. I do some quick breathing exercises to push it back down. It's just your hormones making you paranoid, Clare. Get it together.

I decide to get a bottle of red and a bottle of white. After paying, I place all my goodies in my tote bag and sling it over my shoulder.

I stroll down Corso Italia, heading back toward my bike, unhurried. I linger at shop windows, letting my eyes wander, waiting for something, anything, to tempt me inside. My fingers trail across a vibrant shirt on a sale rack, and I glance at the shop's glass.

That's when I see him.

Reflected in the window, the same weaselly man from the supermarket.

My breath catches. I spin around, but he's gone.

Vanished.

A chill runs down my spine. My heart kicks into overdrive, dredging up that old, primal panic, the kind I haven't felt since the Wild Dogs used to hunt me down at lunchtime.

I hitch my tote bag higher on my shoulder and break into a run, ducking into the first side street I find. My feet pound the pavement as I zigzag through alleyways, taking sharp, random turns, left, right, another left, trying to shake whatever shadow I imagine behind me. Every few steps, I throw a glance over my shoulder.

Nothing.

Still, adrenaline courses through me like fire. I don't know where I'm going anymore, just that I have to keep moving. By the time I stumble into a small piazza with a statue at its centre surrounded by trees, my heart is thundering and my ears ring with the rush of blood. I head for a cluster of palm trees by the ocean, using my old trick of keeping my back safe, I keep a palm tree and the water behind me. When I'm confident I've not been followed here, I rush to the telephone booth across the piazza, slide in a phone card and dial the villa.

Chapter 12

'Luca,' I cry breathlessly when he picks up. 'Someone is after me, I'm being followed.'

'Where are you?' he asks, his voice urgent.

'I don't know,' I sob.

'What can you see?' He prompts.

I scan the street, eyes wide, heart pounding, every shadow suddenly suspicious.

'I'm in a piazza by the water. With my back to the sea, the Hotel Tramontano is on my left.'

'Si, I know it,' he replies. 'Hide, don't come out until you see my car, understand?'

'Yes,' I whimper. 'Please, hurry.' Hanging up the phone, I retreat to the palm trees.

A sharp screech of tires on cobblestones jolts me, and Luca's car skids to a halt. He leaps out, eyes scanning frantically in every direction, his face etched with panic.

'Clare?' he calls.

I rush from my hiding place and run to him. He scoops me into his arms. I sob, deep, heavy sobs into his chest.

'I. Was. So. Scared.' I gulp.

'It's okay, you're safe. You're safe,' he repeats, maybe trying to convince himself as much as me. 'Let's get you home.' Luca scoops me up, carrying me and my groceries, placing us safely into his car. Seeing my possum in a headlight stare, he takes the seatbelt, pulls it across my shoulder, and places it between my breasts, clicking it at my hip. As he stands, he puts a gentle kiss on the top of my head. He gets in, starts the car and drives us slowly home, checking the car mirrors often for anyone on our tail.

Back at the villa, Luca leads me by the hand around the side and through the lemonaia to lessen the chances of us bumping into anyone. Nico is in the pool vacuuming as Luca guides me to my room. If he sees us or has any thoughts on what was going on, he doesn't show it. Luca opens my door, closing it gently behind us. He sits me down on my bed, dropping to his knees, and he slides the sandals off my feet before tossing them aside.

'Stand up,' he directs.

Robotically, I do as he says. He lifts my cotton dress over my head. Tossing it aside, he pulls back my covers.

'Get into bed.'

I do as he says unquestioningly.

He covers my near-nakedness with the cool sheet and heavy duvet. Immediately, I feel safer, and the knot of anxiety in my chest starts to loosen a little. Luca perches on the bed beside me. Slowly, he rubs from between my eyes, back up and over my forehead, just the way my mum used to when I was a toddler and wouldn't give in to sleep.

'You're safe. You're safe. You're safe,' he repeats as he rubs. The adrenaline slowly leaves my body, and suddenly I'm exhausted. I can't keep my eyes open.

I drift into a dreamless sleep.

I don't hear Luca leave, go back to his room or make a phone call to his father.

Chapter 13

Monday 21st July - 9 am

Luca knocks twice on our adjoining door. 'A walk?' he says hopefully when I open it.

'A walk would be nice,' I reply, thinking it will give me time alone with him to ask some questions. 'Give me 5 minutes to change.'

It's a little cooler this morning, and rain threatens as we pound the narrow road that leads to a path through a wooded area.

'About yesterday,' I start.

'Yes, I need to apologise,' Luca responds in a way I didn't expect.

'Why do you need to apologise? You saved me!'

'I should have warned you it might happen,' he looks guilty as hell.

'How could you know?' I demand.

'Why do you think Mario gave you the only orange motorini in Sorrento?' He stops walking, grabbing my arm to stop me also.

'Cause he hates me?' I ask, confused.

'No, it's so everyone in the family knows where you are,' Luca explains. 'So whoever sees you can report back where you are, or where you've been. Where you've shopped, who you've spoken to. Mario wants to know everything. Yesterday, when an Aunty phoned him and said you'd just driven by her house alone, he sent my cousin Davide to follow you.'

'The weasly looking man? That's your cousin?' Poor Davide missed out on the good family genes.

'A little harsh, he's only 21, he might get better looking,' Luca shrugs, not looking too hopeful.

'If you knew it was your cousin, why did you rescue me then?' I ask.

'I didn't know, Clare. I thought it could have been a rival family out to do you harm. Regardless, you sounded so scared. I had to come.' He lowers his gaze, but not enough that I can't see the sadness in his face.

'Were you scared, Luca?'

'*Si*,' he raises his face. In the corner of his eye, a tear glints.

Luca lifts his hand and gently places it beneath my chin, tilting my face toward his.

'I care about you, Clare,' he says, voice low. 'But caring about you and being part of my family… they don't mix.'

His mouth lowers toward mine, the space between us vanishing. Our breath tangles, warm, intimate, full of everything unsaid. Then he closes the distance, pressing his body softly into me as his lips meet mine in a kiss so tender it stills the world.

It's not about desire. It's about tenderness and caring.

The emotion of it blindsides me. Panic flares. I pull back suddenly, breaking the moment.

Chapter 13

'We should get back,' I say quickly, turning away and heading down the trail, my heart thundering louder than my footsteps.

Thursday

The past few days have been a whirlwind, one tour group in, then out, and then another arrival hot on their heels. Another couple of passports were stolen, then miraculously returned and one trip to the hospital with a girl who drank a few too many sambuca shots. After a quick stomach pump, she was fine and on her way. Between the chaos, a couple of visits from burly men delivering unmarked envelopes to Luca, and the familiar soundtrack of Maria and Anna shouting cheerfully at each other as they work, it's been nonstop.

Luca finally corners me when we're alone. His voice is low, urgent.

'I need to talk to you.'

'Okay. Here?' I ask, looking around the atrium.

'No, let's go to the lemonaia, it'll be quiet there.' He leads me out the front doors and around the side of the building.

We sit side by side on the wide window ledge, sun warm on our backs, a soft breeze keeping us cool.

'What's up?' I ask.

'I need to take you away this weekend,' Luca says.

I blink, thrown.

'What if I don't want to go?'

'You have to. My father's called a family conference. Everyone's coming here.'

'And?' I frown, not following what that has to do with me.

'And you can't be here. You mustn't see or hear anything,' he says, firm.

'Your family is weird. No offence.'

Luca turns to me, eyes searching. 'Clare... haven't you figured it out?'

My brow creases. I slowly shake my head. 'Figured what out?'

'My family is mafiosa. My father is the don.'

He watches my face.

In a rush, everything clicks into place: the selective restaurants, the men watching me, the envelopes of cash arriving. The cancelled functions. Not having any outside guests. Paola vanishing after I asked too many questions, only to be replaced by Luca. To keep an eye on me, obviously.

My stomach turns.

All those moments... Were they real?

Or just a way to keep me distracted, to keep me quiet?

'And the villa?' I ask.

'Used to launder money from racketeering,' he hangs his head. 'Things are happening. Bad things, and my family need to talk about what to do.'

'Like worse than laundering money?' I ask.

'Yes. Davide has vanished. We think it's the Graziano family. They are trying to claim some of our turf and have taken Davide as leverage. For now, it's Davide, next,' he shrugs, 'who knows. That's what the meeting is for.'

Chapter 14

Saturday 26th July - 10 am

The rest of Thursday and all of Friday passed in a blur. My body went through the motions, chatting with tour manager Liza, exchanging jokes with Stoney the driver, smiling for the passengers, scribbling notes in the diary about upcoming itineraries. I nodded, responded, and even laughed at the right moments.

But inside, I wasn't present.

My mind was somewhere else entirely, looping back through every detail since I arrived at the villa, replaying it all through a new, sharper lens. Every seemingly harmless moment now shimmered with something darker: the careful way Luca had steered me away from questions, the silent exchanges between him and the men with envelopes, the careful placement of trust.

How much of it was real?

How much of him was real?

I'd told him I wasn't going away with him.

I meant it.

But somehow, here I am, zipping up an overnight bag, loading it into the back of his car. I slide into the low passenger seat, the door closing with a quiet finality. As the engine hums to life, I realise I'm not sure if I'm leaving danger or heading straight into it.

'Where are we going?' I ask, sliding my sunglasses into place to avoid direct eye contact.

'The Eternal City,' Luca says, grinning. 'Roma. It's only about a three-hour drive.'

I keep my expression flat, giving him nothing. Sensing he won't get much conversation, he flicks on the radio. An operatic wail bursts through the speakers, high, dramatic, and utterly jarring. I shift uncomfortably in my seat. Without missing a beat, he turns the volume up.

We travel in silence; the loud opera makes it impossible to speak anyway, as Luca speeds north along the coast, joining the E45 autostrada. He weaves in and out of traffic at speed. I'm not sure if he's trying to scare me or if it's just the way he drives on motorways. I close my eyes and pretend it and the opera aren't happening. Like I used to when I was at primary school and hiding from the bullies, I find a happy place, deep inside my mind.

I wake with a start to a loud screeching noise. I glance around nervously, anticipating an impending crash. There are no cars nearby, and the noise seems to be coming from our own. I glance at my watch, nearly midday. He must've turned the opera music off when I fell asleep.

'What's that noise?' I ask.

'I don't know, but it doesn't sound good. I'm going to pull off here and check it out.'

He whips the car to the right following a sign for 'Cassino'. No sooner do we leave the motorway onto a country road, when the car engine splutters, then stops. With no power, Luca puts his foot on the clutch, moves the gearstick to neutral and guides the car off to the side of the road and safely to a stop.

'Vaffanculo.' He shouts, whacking his fist angrily on the steering wheel. Leaping out of the car, he moves to the bonnet, lowering his hand towards it. 'Cavolo! That's hot. I can't open it to see what's going on. We will have to wait.'

'Great,' I mutter. 'A night away on the side of a country lane, exactly what I need for a night I didn't want to be away in the first place.'

'Come,' he says, taking positive action. 'We will walk to find a garage.'

'I'll wait here,' I sulk.

'I'm not leaving you here,' he's firm.

'Your weird family and the other weird family aren't here. I'll be fine.'

Luca moves around the car and opens my door. 'Out,' he demands.

'No,' I shuffle away from him.

'Yes,' he moves towards me. Before I know it, his hands are on my waist and he's tickling me. I can't help it; laughter erupts from my unwilling mouth. I wriggle, trying to escape his tickle torture.

'Stop,' I beg between giggles. 'I can't breathe.'

'So you'll come?' he asks, smiling.

'Alright, you win. I'll come for a stupid walk.'

I perch on a chair in the mechanics' waiting room as Luca talks to a man in greasy overalls.

'He's just going to pick up the car with his tow truck. I'm going with him. You wait here, we won't be long,' Luca tells me.

'Oh, so it's okay to leave me alone here,' I cast my arm around to show my distaste, 'but not on the side of the road. Makes perfect sense.'

True to his word, they aren't long. Before long, a tow truck rumbles into the forecourt with the Spider hitched behind it. The mechanic hops out, unhooks the car, pops the bonnet, and starts poking around. He fires off questions to Luca in rapid Italian, grunts at the answers, then dives back under the hood.

After a few minutes, he straightens up, wipes his hands on a rag, and heads to the sink to wash up.

'There's good news and bad news,' Luca says, turning to me. 'Which do you want first?'

'The good,' I reply, without hesitation.

'It's the fuel pump, and he can fix it.' Luca flashes a smile.

'And the bad?'

'He needs to order a part, it won't arrive until tomorrow, and that's if he can get his brother to do him a favour on the weekend. So...' he takes a cautious step back, 'we're stuck here for the night.'

'And where exactly is here?' I ask, folding my arms.

'Oh, but wait, more good news,' Luca adds, upbeat. 'Luigi's sister runs a B&B in the town. He says she has room tonight and he can drop us there now.'

I sigh, defeated. 'Great. Let's go.'

I'm wedged between Luca and Luigi in the cramped cab of the tow truck as we rattle our way up Via Pinchera, a winding road that snakes above the town of Cassino, clinging to the slopes of Montecassino. My linen shorts offer little coverage. One thigh brushes against Luigi's rough overalls; the other is pressed against the bare, warm skin of Luca's leg. I try not to think about either.

'This is it,' Luca translates Luigi's words as the tow truck comes to a halt. 'He says his sister won't be home until 7 pm, but we can leave our stuff by the back door and it will be safe.'

Luca opens the cab door. 'Grazie, Luigi.'

Luca leaps gracefully out of the cab onto the dusty road. He extends his hands to help me down before grabbing our two bags from the truck deck.

'This is nice,' he says cheerily as Luigi disappears in the distance.

I can see why Luca's confident our stuff will be safe, this narrow country road doesn't exactly scream high traffic.

'This is cute,' he says, nudging open the gate to a small ochre-coloured cottage with his hip. 'I'll drop our bags, then how about a walk into Cassino for something to eat?'

'Sure,' I grunt, unable to hide the edge in my voice. I know I'm being surly, but I can't help it. I like plans.

Structure.

Control.

This, being stranded in the middle of nowhere with no warning, is the opposite of that, and it grates.

'Come on, Clare,' Luca says gently, clearly reading both my discomfort and my mood. 'This could actually be fun… if you let it.'

We head downhill along Via Pinchera, the road flanked by low stone walls and shaded by a canopy of mature trees. The silence between us isn't exactly comfortable, but it's not strained either, just quiet. Within fifteen minutes, we've reached the base of the hill, and not long after, a line of restaurants comes into view, their tables spilling onto the pavement in the warm evening light.

'Which one do you like the look of?' Luca asks, glancing at me.

'You choose. That's how it works, right?' I shoot back, my words sharper than intended.

'Only in Sorrento,' he says gently. 'Here, you get to decide.'

I exhale, trying to match his effort.

'What about this one?' I nod toward a trattoria with an awning stretched over a handful of sidewalk tables. The red-and-white checked tablecloths catch the breeze, and there's a clear view of a park just across the road. It looks relaxed. Simple. Safe.

Luca orders an antipasto plate and a carafe of white wine while we scan the menus. When the waiter returns with the starter, the wine, and tall glasses of aqua frizzante, I settle on the spaghetti carbonara, and Luca chooses a steak. He pours the wine, the pale liquid catching the last of the daylight, then lifts his glass, waiting for me to do the same.

'To a fun night,' he says, his eyes holding mine as our glasses touch with a soft clink.

I take a long sip, the cold wine instantly taking the edge off.

Maybe this isn't as out of control as it feels.

We have food.

We have shelter.

We even have wine.

The car will be fixed tomorrow and we'll be back at the villa.

For now, I let myself breathe.

I take another sip, longer this time. When I set my glass down, Luca refills it without hesitation.

'Luca?'

'*Sì*, Clare,' he says, smiling gently.

'Is it stressful?'

Chapter 14

He frowns slightly. 'Is what stressful?'

'When I was bullied by the Wild Dogs in primary school,' I begin, 'it was awful, but I always knew there'd be an end. I knew high school would be different; I hoped it would be better. But your life... your family... It's like the conflict never stops. How do you live with that?'

He leans back, thinking.

'I guess I've never known anything else. It's in the air I grew up breathing, don't trust too easily, watch your back, avoid the wrong places, the wrong people.'

I study him. 'Do you want kids one day?'

His gaze flickers to mine, but he doesn't answer. Instead, he takes a long drink and turns to look out at the park across the road, like the answer might be hiding there in the trees.

When our food arrives, we dive in like we haven't eaten in days. Every bite tastes better than the last, hunger sharpening everything. Luca orders a second carafe of wine, and we let the conversation drift to safer, sillier ground, travel disasters, bad first dates, weird tour guests. By the time we're pouring from the third carafe, there's more laughter than talk, our cheeks flushed and eyes bright, the earlier tension melting into the night air.

We pay the bill and start the walk home. It's harder this time, uphill and a little drunk, but soon enough we're through the gate of the B&B.

'Where are our bags?' I ask, casting my eyes around in the dim light.

'Probably right where I left them... here,' Luca points to a spot by the door that most definitely does not have any bags. 'Maybe Luigi's sister took them inside?' He says hopefully, knocking at the door.

'*Buonasera*,' a thickset middle-aged woman greets us when she opens the door. 'Luca? *Si accomodi*.' She steps aside to let us into a small anteroom.

As I admire the floral wallpaper that has possibly been in place since the 1950s, Luca and Luigi's sister has a conversation.

'So,' Luca says when they've finished. 'She says when she got home, there were no bags outside.'

'WHAT?' I screech. Can this trip get any worse? While I've got my travel make-up supplies in my tote bag, my toilet bag with my toothbrush, toothpaste and deodorant was in my overnight bag. Along with a change of clothes and underwear. Underwear, fuck.

'It's okay, we can make do,' Luca soothes. 'She wants us to follow her.'

Luigi's sister leads to the end of a narrow hallway. She opens the door, revealing a bedroom with a double bed and not much room for anything else.

'*Bagno privato*,' she points to a door leading off the bedroom. '*La colazione è alle 9:00, dormi bene*.' She turns back down the hall.

'What did she say?' I ask.

'She said, That's the ensuite, breakfast is at 9 am and sleep well.'

He starts to call after Luigi's sister.

'Ask her where the other room is!' I cut him off before he starts.

'That's what I'm going to do, Clare.'

After a quick conversation, Luigi's sister disappears, and Luca and I are left staring at each other.

'So… seems there was a bit of confusion.'

'What confusion?'

Chapter 14

'Luigi thought we were married,' he laughs.

I glare at him.

'Why would he think that?'

'I don't know,' he shrugs. 'Maybe because we were bickering like an old married couple? The reason probably doesn't matter. The thing is, because he thought we were married, he suggested we stay at his sister's, and...'

'Yes...' I encourage him on.

'She only has this one bedroom,' he finishes sheepishly.

'And you didn't think to ask earlier?'

'Did you?' He fires back.

'Touché.' I concede. 'Do we have any options?'

'Let's recap. It's 8 pm. We have no transport. We have no luggage. We are at least a 30-minute walk from anywhere else. I'd say we have no options. What do you think?'

I hate to agree with him, but he's right.

'Okay, but there's going to be a wall of pillows down the middle of the bed. And no funny business!'

'I'm a gentleman, Clare. Of course.'

Chapter 15

'This is a nightmare,' I sit on the side of the bed, pondering our predicament.

'Which bit?' Luca asks, laughing.

'I've got no clean underwear for tomorrow, let alone clothes.' I look down, pondering.

My navy cotton shirt and linen shorts can hang up and air out overnight, but my underwear?!

'Here's what we are going to do. Do you want a shower?' I ask.

'*Si*,' he confirms.

'Okay. You have a shower, while I make the bed... safe... Then I'll have a shower and handwash my underwear. They should be dry by morning in this heat. By the time I get out of the shower, you need to be asleep. Deal?'

'I'll try my best,' Luca says, heading into the ensuite and closing the door.

While the water runs, I pull back the duvet and top sheet, then place two pillows down the centre of the mattress.

Chapter 15

There.

Barrier established.

I slip off my sandals and tuck them neatly beside the lone chair in the corner, the room's only other piece of furniture.

'I left you plenty of hot water,' Luca says, stepping out of the small bathroom. A towel slung over one shoulder, his clothes draped over the other arm, he's wearing only chambray cotton boxers. Droplets cling to his back, catching the light as he turns to place his clothes neatly on the chair.

'Thanks,' I say, already feeling flustered. 'Now go to sleep,' I command as I close and lock the ensuite door behind me. I hang my shirt and shorts on hooks on the back of the door to air before removing my bra and panties, placing them in the sink, and filling it with water. Adding soap to the mix, I swish my garments around, putting extra soap on the gusset of my panties and rubbing the fabric together. Satisfied they are clean enough, I rinse, wring, and then hang them over the shower rail before ducking into the shower. I turn the cold tap to full, letting an icy stream of water hit my body to rinse away today. I linger to give Luca enough time to get to sleep.

I towel off quickly, then wrap the small bath towel tightly around my chest. Heart ticking faster than I'd like, I flick off the bathroom light and ease the door open. The bedroom is cloaked in silver-blue moonlight, filtering through the sheer curtain of the small window. I step carefully, each movement deliberate, silent.

A shadowy shape rises on one side of the bed, a body-sized mound beneath the sheets. I move to the other side, my bare feet whispering against the floor. Holding my breath, I lift the sheet, let the towel slip to the floor, and slide soundlessly into bed.

Lying on my back, I stare up at the ceiling, every nerve on high alert. I listen to the stillness, to Luca's breathing, searching for the slow, steady rhythm that means he's asleep. Only then, inch by inch, do I begin to relax.

'Clare,' he says. My body tenses immediately, and fight or flight mode kicks in.

'You're supposed to be asleep!' I scold.

'It's not even 9 pm. Can I at least give you a kiss goodnight? Just on the forehead,' he adds.

A kiss on the forehead seems safe enough. 'And then you'll go to sleep?'

'*Sì.*'

'Permission to cross the barrier, granted. Temporarily,' I add, closing my eyes.

The mattress dips as Luca shifts toward me. His chest hair brushes my shoulder, sending a shiver darting through me, settling low and deep. Oh god. Granting that request might've been a mistake.

His lips press softly between my eyebrows, at the lower end of my forehead, but still acceptably on my forehead. They lift, then return to the same spot with agonising gentleness. I inhale, and the scent of his clean, sun-warmed skin fills me. It's dizzying.

He kisses me again, this time on the tip of my nose. Still technically the face, and still kind of within acceptable range, I tell myself.

My pulse doesn't care about logic.

Then… nothing.

His lips hover, somewhere too close. I hold my breath, torn between two impossible urges: to pull away or for those kisses to keep moving south.

Still, I don't open my eyes.

Chapter 15

I can't.

I'm frozen, not from fear, but anticipation.

Then his lips graze mine, another pause, perhaps to see if I chastise him.

I don't. I can't.

His mouth moves back to mine, and this time it settles. My body betrays me, and I open my mouth, welcoming his tongue.

'Oh, Clare, he groans against my skin, his mouth now trailing down the curve of my cheek. His lips find my earlobe, pulling it gently between them, his tongue flicking in a way that sends sparks straight through me.

Then he pulls back, rising up over me.

In the soft glow of moonlight, he grips the top of the duvet and sheet. Slowly, deliberately, he begins to draw them down, his eyes locked on mine, watching for the slightest sign of hesitation.

He pauses just as the covers reach the tops of my breasts, giving me a moment to stop him.

I don't.

With one smooth motion, he slides them down to my waist.

He takes my right hand, lifts it above my head, and holds it there, his other hand quickly claiming my left. Now both wrists are pinned beneath his, my body bare, exposed, and completely at his mercy.

And I let him. Heart racing, breath shallow, I surrender to the thrill of trust and the danger of wanting.

The kissing resumes, mouth to mouth, then slower, deeper, down my neck and across my chest. He turns his head, trailing soft kisses along the curve of my breast before taking a nipple into his mouth, teasing it the same way he did my earlobe.

'Oh God,' I moan, barely breathing.

He moves to the other breast, pulling the nipple gently between his teeth. He frees one hand, places it on the nipple he's just left, rolling it between his fingers.

Just as I begin to unravel, his mouth continues its descent, kisses across my ribs, down my stomach, stopping just at the edge of my pubic hair. He can't go lower without freeing my hands. When he does, I immediately bury them in his hair, tugging, then pushing him down, urging him on.

The first graze of his stubbled cheek against my inner thigh steals my breath. Then his tongue begins, slow, steady, devastating.

He brings me to the edge and pulls back.

Again.

Again.

'Please,' I whisper, desperate.

This time, he doesn't stop. My back arches. The moan that rips from me is raw, rising from somewhere deep and primal. Luca lifts a hand, gently pressing it over my mouth.

'Luigi's sister will think I'm murdering you,' he murmurs with a crooked smile, before crawling back up the bed and silencing me with a kiss.

'Have you got protection?' I ask.

'From the mob?' he replies.

'So we can have sex.' Silently, I roll my eyes.

'*Si*.' He jumps up, retrieves his wallet from his shorts pocket and pulls from it a foil wrapper. 'Are you sure?' He asks.

'I'm sure.'

'You know that I'll never hurt you, Clare?' He asks earnestly.

'I know,' I say. And I really do.

He rips open the foil, slides the condom on and moves to hover above me.

Chapter 15

'Really sure?'

I take him in my hand and guide him. I'm really sure.

Chapter 16

Sunday

It's 3 pm by the time Luigi has the car finished, and the drive back to the villa takes over two hours. Luca is several hundred thousand lira lighter for having a mechanic work on a Sunday.

'I hope your dad pays for the repairs,' I say, as we roll slowly down the driveway.

'*Forse, forse no*,' he says, shrugging.

'Speak of the devil.'

Mario waits on the front steps of the villa for us, arms crossed, looking none too pleased.

Mario approaches the car when we stop. He and Luca have a tense exchange before Moretti senior says, 'I need to speak to both of you, inside.'

I look at Luca for translation on the bit before he switched to English.

'He just asked where the fuck we've been, he's said been waiting for us.'

'Why does he want to speak to both of us?' I ask.

Chapter 16

Luca shrugs, then vaults over his door, comes around to mine and opens it for me.

'Whatever it is, we can handle it.' He plants a quick kiss on the top of my head.

'In here,' Mario directs us into the bar. He closes the door behind us as we take a seat at a circular table.

'What's up, Mario?' I decide to front-foot whatever is coming.

'We had the family conference,' Mario states. 'At this conference, everyone in the family shared information that they had. We also have someone on the inside of the Grazione family, so we get an insight into their operations.'

'Okay,' I say, confused about how this affects me.

'This is what we know,' Mario continues. 'Last week, I had Davide follow you.'

'That was unnecessary, but I know.'

'You don't KNOW what is necessary here, Clare,' Mario flares.

'*Papa*, please, *parla con calma*,' Luca encourages his father.

'What we didn't know was that the Grazione family was following Davide. They're trying to move in on some of our business, and they thought if they could take one of our people, they could put pressure on us. When you evaded Davide, they split their people; one followed you, the rest followed Davide,' Mario pauses.

'You mean a rival mob family were following me?' I ask, stunned.

If my anxiety skyrocketed with one mob family on my tail, I can't imagine my state if I'd known there was more than one after me. Nervously, I rub my tattoo.

'*Fanculo*,' Luca mutters.

'*Si, fanculo*,' Mario confirms. 'That's when they took Davide. They were going to take you too, Clare, but Luca turned up like

Superman and scooped you up.'

'Not good,' Luca says.

'What do you mean, not good?' I ask, bewildered and a little hurt. 'You saved me, that's good, right?'

'He means it's not good because now the Grazione's know that Luca is in love with you,' Mario states.

'What?' I protest. 'Luca's not in love with me.'

I look at Luca.

He looks away, embarrassed.

'Anyone with one eye can see that Luca is in love with you,' Mario says. 'And that puts you in danger, Clare.' Mario turns to Luca, 'I told you to watch her, not fall in love with her stupido.'

'If they so much as lay a finger on her,' Luca growls at Mario, his voice shaking with fury, 'I swear to God, I'll burn both families to the ground.'

'See?' Mario says, turning back to me. 'Now they know that Luca reacts with emotion, they will use you to get to Luca. You are putting the entire Moretti family at risk.'

My heart sinks. The last thing I want is for Luca, or his weird family, to get hurt.

'What do I need to do?' I ask.

'Leave,' Mario says coldly. 'Tomorrow. There's a flight from Naples to Melbourne at 10 am. Luca will drive you. After that, you do not speak again. Ever. Understood?'

I nod, slowly, the weight of it all settling on my chest.

Tears blur my vision, spilling over in silent surrender.

'What about Terrific Tours? My job?' I whisper, my voice cracking.

'I've spoken to Carlos,' Mario says. 'He knew exactly what the company was getting into when he signed the contract. What he didn't count on was you being smart enough to put the pieces together.' He pauses, watching me carefully. 'He knows you're going back to Australia. He said you're welcome to return next summer, and he'll even make you a hotel manager. Somewhere else.'

'And Luca? Will you stay here?' I turn my tear-streaked face to him, but it's Mario who answers.

'Luca's going away for a while, until things cool off with the Grazione family. And in case anything happens to me,' he says firmly. 'He's a terrible receptionist anyway. Paola will come back and run the desk.'

Relief flickers through me, Paola's alive, not… disposed of, Luca was telling the truth about that. But sadness settles in just as quickly. Luca's life, once again, isn't his own. He's being moved like a pawn in his father's game of chess.

'It's okay,' Luca says, laying his hand gently over mine. 'It's my duty.'

9 pm

Luca sits silently on my bed, watching as I fold clothes and pack them neatly into my suitcase. The mood is heavy, and for a long time, neither of us speaks. I set aside tomorrow's outfit and tuck the last few items from the wardrobe into the case.

I place the suitcase on the floor and move to Luca, positioning myself in front of him, standing between his knees.

'Luca?'

He lifts his eyes from the floor, sorrow swimming in their depths. I cradle his face in my hands and press my lips to his. The kiss is slow, aching, full of everything we can't say. But grief shifts to hunger, and suddenly we're clinging to each other like we're drowning.

Between kisses, Luca tugs my T-shirt over my head; I do the same to his.

He peels my shorts down over my hips, and I let them fall, stepping out as our mouths stay locked.

My bra releases behind my back with a practised flick of his fingers, then I toss it aside.

His hands slide beneath the waistband of my underwear, dragging them down until I take over, breathless.

He stands, and I unbuckle his belt with trembling hands. His shorts and boxers fall in one swift motion. He pulls me into him, spins us, and we tumble onto the bed, tangled and urgent.

Our lovemaking is fierce, wordless, driven by the knowledge that we don't have long together.

When it's over, we lie still, side by side, hearts racing and breaking at once.

I turn onto my side, caressing his chest hair, then tracing my hand down his abdomen to his belly button and back up. Luca tilts his head to the side, giving me a glazed, post coital smile.

'You could come with me,' I blurt out.

'What?' He's stunned.

'Come with me, Luca. You need to get away until things cool down. Why can't that be in Melbourne?'

'Papa would not allow it,' he says, resigned to his fate. 'You don't understand, Clare, Papa is in real danger with this feud. If anything happens to him, I need to be nearby. If he dies, I am the Don.'

'Not if you don't want to be,' I whisper.

But I know this is a battle I can't win. If this is our last night together, I want to remember every second.

My hand trails slowly down his torso, fingers brushing the lines of his stomach. This time, I don't stop at his belly button. I circle the tip of him, teasing, stroking languidly until he begins to harden beneath my touch. I shift lower, replacing my hand with my mouth, taking my time, savouring him.

'Oh, Clare...' he groans, his voice low and rough with want. I glance up, he's watching me, eyes dark with heat and heartbreak.

'Kiss me,' he murmurs, half-sitting, hands slipping beneath my arms to pull me up his body.

I straddle him, and we kiss, deep, slow, aching. There's no urgency now, just the desperate need to feel everything, to make this count. When we're both ready, I guide him inside me, rocking gently, drawing out every wave of sensation. Our rhythm is unhurried, reverent. When release takes us, it crashes like a tide, pleasure and grief tangled together. We cry out, clinging to each other as if we can hold back morning with our bodies alone.

As I drift off to sleep, Luca whispers in my ear, 'I love you, Clare.'

Chapter 17

November 22nd - Melbourne - 9 am

For approximately the 117th day in a row, my first thought when I wake is of Luca. I glance around my small bedroom in Carlton, wishing I were back in the stables in Sorrento. As always, I shake the thought away. Monday to Friday, it's easier to be distracted, to forget what might have been, as I get dressed and head to my receptionist job at the hotel. I'm hoping for a promotion by Christmas. If I get it, I've almost decided not to go back to Europe next summer. Time to lay down some roots.

Sliding into fluffy slippers, I drag myself to the bathroom for a quick shower. I wash my hair, then pull on jeans and a t-shirt.

'Anyone awake?' I call out into the hallway.

'In the kitchen,' comes the reply.

I join my flatmates for a Saturday planning session over a hot drink, coffee to sniff, and tea to actually drink. The perfect combo.

'Nicky, Toni! Are you coming to the mall or what?' I shout down the hallway a couple of hours later.

Chapter 17

'Nick's in the bathroom,' Toni calls back. 'Then it's my turn, then we're good.'

My return to Melbourne, while unplanned, was perfectly timed. The flatmate who moved in after I left in July had a breakdown and moved back home. Not great for her, obviously, but it meant I could slot straight back into my old life, same flat, same friends, same city. The job is secure, easy, and dull. No hot Italian beside me, no burly men dropping off wads of cash, no looming threat.

'Hurry up!' I yell again.

'You've got so impatient,' Nicky grumbles.

'Is that the Italian influence?' Toni teases.

We pile into my trusty green Mazda. I turn the key and she starts first try.

'What kind of car did your Italian fling drive again?' Nicky asks.

'A black Alfa Romeo Spider,' I say, smiling at the memory. 'One he rebuilt himself, with his own hands.' I get a tingle remembering what those hands could do to my body. I pause. 'And it wasn't a fling. It was... more than that.' I trail off, unsure how to explain.

'Have you heard from him?' Toni asks gently.

'How? I didn't give him my number. And his father made it clear, no contact.'

'Classic daddy issues,' Nicky mutters.

The truth is, I've thought about calling the villa almost every day. Wondered if Paola would pass on a message or give me a number. But I couldn't risk putting Luca, or any of his bizarre family, in danger.

'Do you think if an Italian mob boss got murdered, it'd make the news here?' I ask suddenly.

'What the hell?' Nicky turns to me. 'Where did that come from?'

While I'd told them a lot about Luca, I hadn't shared the whole story. I'm not even sure why. Maybe it sounds too far-fetched.

'No reason.'

I slow for a red light, glancing in my rear-view mirror.

'That car's coming in hot,' I say.

Nicky and Toni look over their shoulders just in time to see a red Toyota slam into the back of the Mazda. We're jolted forward, our seatbelts snapping us back into place.

'Is everyone okay?' Nicky asks.

'Just got a fright,' Toni says, wide-eyed.

'Yeah,' I say, moving my head side to side to check my neck.

I step out and walk to the back. There's a sizeable dent in the Mazda, but my tow bar's done more damage to the Toyota's front. Both cars are still drivable. I march toward the Toyota's driver door, ready to go full mobster. Horns blare behind us as traffic crawls past, rubbernecking.

The door opens and out steps a frail, grey-haired woman, clearly shaken.

'I'm so sorry, dear,' she says, taking my hands in her trembling ones. 'I don't know what happened. I just didn't see you.'

I want to rage, demand how she missed a stationary car in broad daylight. But instead I say, 'It's okay. Accidents happen.'

'Let me get a piece of paper and give you my contact and insurance details. I'll also give you the name of my grandson's garage. He's very good, his name's George,' she smiles weakly.

As she scribbles in a small notebook pulled from her handbag, I wonder if this is some con to drum up business for her grandson. Not very cost-effective, I decide.

'There you go, dear. The garage is on Nicholson Street, not

far. He's open Saturdays if you want to go now. He has my insurance details. It's not my first oopsie lately,' she rambles. 'My family wants me to give up my licence, but I can't imagine not being able to get to bingo. Sorry again about this.'

I help her back into her car. 'Drive safe now,' I say as she closes the door, reverses slowly around my car, then nearly runs the red light.

Chapter 18

'Not quite what we'd planned for our weekend,' I say once I'm back in the car.

'Did you give her what for?' Toni demands.

'Couldn't. She was a sweet old lady. One who definitely shouldn't be on the road, but is sweet all the same. She gave me the address of her grandson's garage on Nicholson Street. How about we stop in there? If he needs time to look at the car, we can leave it and score some free parking, then walk to Lygon Court to shop. What do you think?'

'Sounds good,' says Nicky. 'Will be easier than trying to sort it during the week, when you've got work.'

Like she hasn't just been shunted, the trusty Mazda starts without complaint. I put her in gear, wait for the next green light, and head toward the garage.

'What are you shopping for?' Toni asks.

'I'm on the lookout for a new gym outfit,' Nicky responds. 'Time to retire the g-string leotard. Thinking maybe Lycra shorts or something with less... chafe.'

Chapter 18

'R.I.P. the thong,' Toni laughs. 'I need a new skirt for work, and maybe a blouse, and maybe a jacket.'

Toni is a shopaholic. Making sure she doesn't spend her rent money will be our top priority.

'There it is,' Nicky shouts, pointing to a hand-painted sign that reads 'George's Garage.'

I pull the Mazda onto the forecourt and cut the engine.

'I won't be long,' I promise.

We all get out. Nicky and Toni lean against the hood, watching me walk towards the open garage doors. Inside, a classic car sits in pieces to one side. On the other, a late-model Honda waits with a deep dent in its driver's door.

The space smells of metal and dust, but something else lingers, coffee, maybe, and a familiar, faint citrus smell I can't quite place.

A radio murmurs in the background.

'Hurry up,' Toni calls, as I stand at the threshold, nose in the air like a scent will tell me something my brain can't quite catch. 'The shops are waiting.'

'George?' I call, stepping cautiously onto the workshop floor. From somewhere off to the side, maybe a smoko room, I hear humming.

'George?' I say again, louder.

'George is no here,' comes the reply. 'Just a minute.'

My heart jolts.

No.

Surely I'm imagining it.

Is that really the voice I think it is?

It can't be.

How could it?

I lower my gaze to the floor and rub the inside of my wrist, fingers finding the familiar edges of the tattoo. Heavy footsteps approach. Steel-capped boots come into view, a couple of feet from mine.

'He's right there for fuck's sake,' Nicky yells behind me. 'Speak to the man so we can get out of here,' then, quieter, to Toni, 'Jesus, check him out. What a hottie.'

I lift my eyes slowly. Tears spring up before I can stop them.

He steps toward me, tentative, cautious.

I don't stop him.

His hands cup my face, gentle, trembling slightly.

'Clare,' he whispers.

'Luca, I can't believe it's you. How...'

He silences me with a kiss that feels like I'm home.

'Bloody hell,' Toni mutters. 'If I knew this was going to happen, I'd have offered to bring my car today.'

The end.

If you enjoyed Love, Lies & Lemon Trees, please consider leaving a review on Amazon or Goodreads and pick up the others in the series, A Fish Out Of Sparkling Water and Paint Me A Lie.

What Goes On Tour - Chapter 1

London: Departure Day -2

Monday 13th May 1996

'What part of I'M NOT ON THE PILL did you struggle with, Skipper?' I ask, swatting him on the side of his strawberry blond head.

'Sorry... I... uh... Just got carried away.' He at least has the decency to sound sheepish. The small remaining glow from the fumbling bedroom encounter and the preceding nine (ish) large vodka and tonics evaporates like a drop of water on a hot rock. In that split second, I feel deflated and more than a little pissed off.

The trouble with the withdrawal method of contraception is that the sole chance of it working at all revolves around the person who is supposed to 'withdraw' actually doing so. But not only do they need to do it, they need to do it in a timely manner.

Shit, bugger, shit, bugger, shit.

Bugger.

Tomorrow I have to trek from one side of London to the other to go to the office and get, what I can only guess, will be a hauling over the coals for sins on my previous tour around Europe. I need to collect a ton of paperwork and instructions for my next tour, before a 5pm pre-departure meeting. And now, thanks to Skipper, I also have to fit in a visit to the local sleazy 'free for foreigners' doctor. Hopefully I can get the morning after pill without a lecture on the perils of casual sex.

Fan-fucking-tastic.

'Right, you better go then. Big day tomorrow.' I direct Skipper, pushing him off me and over the side of the narrow single bed with one impressive shove.

As he fumbles around the tiny hotel room's grubby carpeted floor for his clothes, I wonder three things:

1. How the hell DID I end up in bed with this guy? The answer to that question probably has something to do with the vodka, and;
2. Why do all coach drivers (you must call them coaches, not buses. Coaches don't stop to pick people up. Being a coach driver is supposedly much more salubrious than driving a bus), have ridiculous names like Skipper? Already I have worked on tours of Europe with a Dipstick, Blue (there is a little and a big one of those; I'd had the little one), Sandfly, Psycho, Boxo and Rasher.
3. What is it going to be like when we are all 80 and reminiscing about old times in Europe? 'Do you remember Russell Jones?' someone would ask. 'Hmmm... was that Sandfly or Rasher?' Bloody madness.

As a tidal wave of exhaustion pummels me, all I want to do is close my eyes and slip into a dream that does not involve accidental pregnancies.

'See you out there somewhere,' says Skipper, as the heavy off-white wooden door closes, clicking locked behind him.

Not if I can help it, I think, as I fall into a deep and thankfully dreamless sleep.

Click HERE to read What Goes On Tour now.

About the Author

Gillian Scott lives at the bottom of the world in beautiful New Zealand, but her heart has always been on the move. Bitten by the travel bug at eighteen, she has spent decades exploring the globe, first as a tour rep and manager in Europe during the 1990s, then leading groups through New Zealand, Australia, Canada, the U.S., India, and, recently, back through Europe, Australia and South America.

In 2011, Gillian, her husband, and their two young children swapped routine for adventure, packing up their lives to backpack around the world for nine unforgettable months.

Drawing on her years behind the microphone of a coach and in front of hundreds of travellers, Gillian turned her experiences into fiction. Her debut series, *What Goes On Tour,* and the follow-up Terrific Tour series capture the humour, heart, and chaos of life on the road, where the stories are as unpredictable as the passengers.

You can connect with me on:

https://gillianscottcreative.com

https://www.facebook.com/GillianScottCreative

https://www.instagram.com/gillianscottcreative

Subscribe to my newsletter:

http://eepurl.com/hHgCfX

Also by Gillian Scott

Feel-good, travel-inspired romantic comedies about characters you'll recognise, root for, and fall in love with.

What Goes On Tour

A laugh-out-loud love triangle romantic comedy aboard a European coach tour.

In the summer of 1996, Sharon "Shaz" Green lands her dream role as a tour leader guiding travellers across Europe. But when a hangover morning reveals she's accidentally slept with a colleague, Shaz's perfectly planned season takes a sharp detour. Enter Roger, her flirtatious co-tour manager—and, even more complicated, Skipper, the charismatic coach driver who's caught in the crossfire.

Now Shaz must juggle quirky tourists, unexpected encounters, and the messy tangle of her heart. Can she maintain her professionalism while pursuing love? Or will the chaos of romance derail her European adventure?

Brimming with humour, heartfelt moments, and a nostalgic 1990s backdrop, *What Goes On Tour* is a must-read for fans of travel romance, women's contemporary fiction, and romantic comedy lovers everywhere.

What Goes On Tour Too, and What Goes On Tour Camping, continue the adventure.

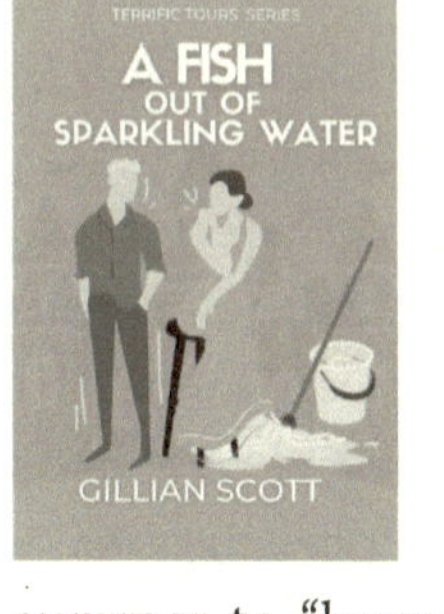

A Fish Out of Sparkling Water

A laugh-out-loud, heart-tugging romantic comedy about finding purpose, falling in love, and learning that the best things in life can't be bought.

Esther Smith's life in South Africa is all champagne and silk sheets — until her father sends her to rural France for the summer to "learn responsibility." Arriving at Château Vin Rouge in designer heels, Esther is horrified to find she's expected to *work*. Scrubbing floors, cooking for guests, and sharing a stable room with strangers were not on her packing list.

Then there's Benji — the maddeningly calm, quietly magnetic Head Cleaner who sees right through her privileged façade. Between disastrous chores, late-night kitchen raids, and a growing connection she never expected, Esther starts to discover who she really is — and what she truly wants.

But when her family calls her home with news that changes everything, Esther must decide whether to return to the life she knew or fight for the one she's fallen in love with.

Warm, funny, and full of heart, A Fish Out of Sparkling Water is a sparkling escape for fans of *Emily Henry, Sophie Kinsella,* and *The Summer I Turned Pretty.*

Paint Me A Lie

A glamorous French Riviera rock star romance about secrets, second chances, and the lies we tell to protect our hearts.

Bella's summer job at a bustling campground in Antibes is hardly five-star, but her nightly escapes to Monaco let her pretend she belongs in that glittering world. Then she meets Jock — a charming Scotsman who claims he's just a house painter helping family nearby.

He's easy-going, funny, and far too good to be true. And as their paths keep crossing under the Riviera lights, Bella starts to suspect Jock's story has more layers than a freshly painted wall. When the truth comes out, it could destroy the fragile trust — and unexpected love — they've built between them.

Paint Me a Lie is a witty, heartfelt romantic comedy about love, deception, and discovering what's real in a world obsessed with appearances. Perfect for fans of *Josie Silver* and *Sophie Kinsella.*

www.ingramcontent.com/pod-product-compliance
Lightning Source LLC
LaVergne TN
LVHW051011080826
845145LV00009B/2575